BENEATH THE MULBERRY TREE

JENNIFER B. DUFFEY

© 2015 Jennifer B. Duffey

Printed in the United States of America

First Printed January 28, 2015

Cover Art by Victoria Hawkins

ISBN: 978-1505624892

For my Mom and the man who loved her.
We miss you, Daddy.

Prologue

Dear Katie,

Libraries are filled with millions of books professing the true nature of love. Poets expound on it. Novelists romanticize it. Cynics deride it. Reference books define it. Yet few truly understand it.

Of these types of love I know nothing.

What I do know of love I learned long ago. The lessons were so subtle and germane to my life at the time; it is only now upon reflection that I begin to realize the power of affection that truly existed. And it's only now that I understand how fortunate my siblings and I were to witness such extraordinary devotion and beauty nestled within the gently swaying pines of home.

You were only a child when all these things happened. You won't remember them as vividly as your cousins. Therefore, I'm sharing this with you now, so that as you grow older, you'll know how amazing their story truly was.

Love,
Mom

Chapter One

JIMMY SIPPED HIS coffee as he watched the fog rolling over the fields. The rhythmic sway of the porch swing in sharp contrast to the herd of elephants stampeding through his stomach. He hadn't slept in over a week. Not since he'd read ol' man Johnson's obituary Wednesday a week ago. And now those few simple paragraphs plagued him with insanity.

It wasn't that he was particularly troubled by Johnson's death. Truth be told, he'd only met the man face to face on two occasions and both instances had been less than positive. The old hermit held fast to a long engrained isolationist policy. He freely ostracized every member of the human race regardless of pedigree. Only his paid housekeeper was permitted to set foot on his hallowed grounds and she was frequently on the verge of exile herself.

So when the announcement of his death appeared, Jimmy read the news with little regard for the man who stood so resolutely against the world. Saying a quick prayer for the old man's soul, he quickly turned the page to read about the improvements underway at the nearby Air Force Base.

That night Jimmy drifted off into a fitful sleep. After kissing his wife on the cheek, he rolled over only to find his eyes stubbornly remained open. They simply refused to close. He didn't feel particularly anxious. Nothing he could put his finger on. Had something happened during the day that he should worry about? No. Not that he could remember. He went back over the events slowly just to make sure. He'd gone to the feed and seed store to get his supplies for his garden. He needed to get things planted within the next week if he had any hope of his corn making a decent crop. He came home and ate lunch with Myrna then repaired the fence around the pasture. After supper, he read the paper and slept through several pitiful examples of television excellence.

With the exception of going to the store, it was the same set of events that unfolded daily since his retirement. Busy but far from stressful.

He readjusted his pillow and drove his head further into it willing his eyes to close. It worked. As his eyelids closed, his mind's eye sprang to life with full vigor. He saw himself walking through a dense patch of woods, down a hill that led to a house. He'd never seen these woods before, at least not that he could remember. As the house came into view, he was startled to see the somewhat neglected abode of ol' man Johnson's. These were his woods behind his house. As Jimmy continued around the home, he realized he was not alone. His friend Bill was with him discussing property values and mortgages.

Jimmy shook himself awake to clear his dreams once more. It made no sense to dream about a house he'd only driven by when he should be thinking about the work he needed to do on his tractor. That was far more essential to planting than some old dilapidated dwelling. That's where his worries should be focused. On the busted fuel line on his Massey Ferguson.

He punched the pillow again in search of more relevant thoughts and drifted off. Once again he saw himself walking around the outside of Johnson's home with Bill, his friend and real estate agent. They were talking about the sale of the home. Somehow Bill looked as dumbfounded as Jimmy felt. On and on the night went. Each dream a graphic detail of property that belonged to Johnson's estate. Each fantasy stirring him further away from quiet rest.

He looked at the clock. 3:18. Almost three hours until the alarm went off. He decided to give sleep one more try. That's when he heard it. A voice as clear as the noon day sky telling him to buy Johnson's land. He turned to find the source, hoping that perhaps Myrna had read his mind and was playing a joke but she lay there lost in slumber.

The whole idea was absurd. The house looked bad from the outside. The lord only knew what it was like on the inside. And it was common knowledge that Johnson had twenty of the most worthless acres on God's green earth. It was a swampy, wooded marshland jutting up to railroad tracks that ran between Byron and Fort Valley. Boxed in except for a small easement beside the old country store that had long since gone out of business. There was no way he would ever consider buying that.

He made a quick trip to the bathroom. He studied his reflection in the mirror for a moment. His dark brown hair had begun showing the signs of age with streaks of gray forming along the edges. Two small indentions on each temple a permanent reminder of the glasses he had worn most of his life. A squared, solid jaw and a small cleft on his chin. He looked more like his father every day, although his father had died more than thirty years ago. He was a sensible man. He always had been. He was never one to make a rash decision, especially where money was concerned. Climbing back in bed, he made a staunch resolution against the very notion of buying Johnson's land.

Every night since that day followed as a faithful twin. Doze off, dream of Johnson's place, wake up, repeat. Listen to the phantom give real estate advice. Ignore. Go to the bathroom. Resolve never to consider buying the land. Lie back down and catnap for a couple of hours. The whole process had left him drained and more than a little disoriented.

The days were proving just as troublesome as the nights. Every project seemed to edge further off kilter. It started that first morning. Repairing the fuel line had been a disaster.

Images of Johnson's place kept creeping into his psyche. He almost stripped the fitting connecting the line to the carburetor. Once he calmed down and finally disconnected the line, he fumbled with the plug and doused himself with gasoline. By lunchtime, he reeked of fuel, sweat, and a fair amount of blood he managed to spill when he smashed his hand reattaching the hose. It had not been his finest morning.

And still the images haunted him.

It took him two whole days to get his seed in the ground. A project that should have taken less than a day lingered on into eternity. First, two of his tiller blades snapped and had to be replaced. Then, once he thought progress was being made, his seeder jammed and dumped half of his corn kernels in a pile. Thankfully, he finally finished seeding before the storm blew in and was able to enjoy a peaceful evening listening to the rain from his porch swing.

Things didn't go much better the following day when he was awaken by the deputy sheriff informing him that half his cows were loose and roaming down Highway 49. They were causing quite a disturbance but fortunately traffic on an early Sunday morning was light and no one had gotten hurt. It took the better part of the morning to get them pinned back in, all without the aid of strong coffee. That afternoon, he found the culprit of the escape – a giant sweet gum tree had fallen during the night destroying a large section of fence. It took a day to repair.

But sleep refused to come.

Now, he sat gazing off into the horizon after the never ending sequence of catastrophes. Nothing had gone right and his patience was gone. Last night for the first time since the dreams started, he began to imagine possible uses for that worthless piece of property. Perhaps he could fix up the house and subdivide the rest of the land into lots. People were always looking to build their own places, especially nowadays. It wasn't an exact plan but at least after he began to make preparations for the land, his fitful nights seemed to subside a bit.

Honestly, he had to admit the whole thing didn't make any sense at all. He'd worked hard all his life. His father taught him how to do masonry and lath work by the age of fourteen. When he was twenty, he followed his dad and uncles across the country looking for work anywhere they could find it. His journeys took him north to New York City, over to Chicago, and as far west as Oklahoma. Times had been tough, but he'd learned the value of a dollar and experience had taught him a dollar was far more valuable in his pocket than thrown away after some fool notion. He'd saved all his life, finally buying a small stonemason business and building it into one of the most successful construction firms in middle Georgia. He was so successful in fact that he was one of the few men he knew who fully retired by the age of fifty-two. And while most other people spent the last night of the '80s with drink and celebration, he was home with Myrna, looking forward to finally spending some time with his family after too many years struggling for financial security. He couldn't wait to start the new decade and enjoy the freedom of retirement.

He loved the life they'd built. They'd bought this place more than a decade ago, slowly making it into the home they'd always wanted. It wasn't much by some people's standards. Only sixty acres. About forty of that was good grazing land for two dozen or so cows. It had plenty of woods to hunt in and a couple of acres to garden each spring. They had more than enough food each year and he had plenty of projects to keep him busy. And he could spend time doing whatever he enjoyed, not worrying about deadlines or new bids. Everything had been perfect for over four years until that damned obituary.

He sipped his coffee and listened to Myrna finishing the breakfast dishes in the kitchen.

He didn't exactly know how he was going to convince her that they needed twenty more acres and another house. After all, that wasn't exactly like going to the store and buying an extra sack of flour. That was a pretty hefty investment. And one guaranteed never to fully pay off. Even if he could make things break even, it would be entirely too much aggravation to have to deal with.

Myrna slid the glass door open and joined him on the swing. "Looks like it'll be a pretty day."

"Yeah, should be real nice if it ain't too hot." He looked down at his cup.

"I think the TV said it was only going to get up to about eighty-five today. Shouldn't be too bad."

They each sipped their coffee, allowing the swing to move of its own accord. Finally, Jimmy broke the silence.

"There's been something I've been wanting to talk to you about."

"What?" Myrna looked over at him as he stared off into the distance.

"You saw that ol' man Johnson died the other day."

"Yeah, I saw that."

"I've been thinking about buying his property."

She wasn't exactly sure what she expected to hear, but that wasn't it. "You have?"

"Yeah."

"Why?"

"Just seems like the right thing to do." He took another sip of his coffee and continued looking out over the pasture.

"Since when?"

"Oh, I've been thinking about it for awhile."

"I didn't even know you wanted it." She knew *she* didn't want it. The fact that he did was news to her.

"Well, I didn't really."

That brought another strange look over the rims of her glasses. "You don't? Then why are you thinking about buying it?"

"It's kinda hard to explain." He took a deep breath and let the story unfold before her. Even saying it aloud seemed crazy.

When he was finished, she nodded her head and pondered the situation for a moment. "But what are we going to do with it if we buy it?"

"I don't know." Jimmy shook his head.

"Well, I don't want it." She said firmly. "We've got just about all we can handle now. You already can't get to everything you want to do and that old house is falling apart at the seams. It'd take forever to fix that up. Plus all the taxes. Each year the county commissioners keep adding on for every little thing."

He couldn't argue with her. Every point she made was correct and another reason why the very idea was sheer lunacy. "You're right." And he vowed to put the idea out of his mind.

As the day wore on, he replayed her words like a tattoo. Myrna always offered sound, sage advice. He couldn't have asked for a better partner to walk through life with. He'd watched so many others who'd married weaker, less capable partners struggle through the hardships of life. He would have never said their life together had been easy, particularly when the babies were little and he had gone out of state to find work, but she'd always been there. His rock and partner. And now, she offered the advice he needed to hear to get these crazy ideas out of his head once and for all.

For over a week, he slept soundly without the first hint of plaguing voices or fractured dreams. His world once again found its solid footing. He went on about the business of running a small farm, tending to the garden, and feeding the cows. Then, as quickly as they had begun before, the intrusive thoughts began again with far more ferocity.

He was standing by the fence at the cow pasture waiting on the water trough to completely fill when he heard someone approach from behind. He turned expecting to find Myrna standing behind him yet he was complete alone except for Curly, his Black Angus bull, and a flock of lady bovines. It was an unsettling feeling but probably just a figment of his imagination. The critters playing in the woods behind him could sometimes sound bigger than they were. It wasn't until he heard the voice, the same voice he'd heard all those nights, that he truly felt unease.

"Buy Johnson's place."

He looked around once more to find he was still alone. He looked at Curly for some form of reassurance but the animal stared blankly back at him as if completely impervious to what had just transpired. Maybe it wasn't an act. Maybe nothing had happened and Jimmy was the one who was going crazy.

He didn't mention the encounter to Myrna at supper that evening. She asked if he had gotten the peas and okra in the ground. He told her the corn had started showing. It looked like that would do fine as long as they got enough rain. She asked what was wrong. After thirty-seven years together, she could tell by the tone of his voice that something was bothering him. It would have been the perfect time to tell her about the voice. To tell her what was happening. But he didn't. It was crazy.

Voices didn't just appear out of thin air. And so, he brushed off the concern as being overly tired. There was nothing to worry about.

That night, the dreams began again. The same cycle as before. The same voice telling him to buy Johnson' place. The same battle within to fight for his sanity. Myrna was right, of course. Buying that property made absolutely no sense. It was poorly positioned really only good for hunting. It had a small fishing pond in the back which Jimmy would have enjoyed visiting on a regular basis but that alone didn't make it a good investment, especially since he was retired and they were now on a fixed income. He had budgeted their savings to see them both comfortably through their golden years together. A major purchase like that would greatly reduce that level of savings. Again he cast the idea off as foolishness.

But as the nights wore on, he noticed that if he concentrated on how to make the purchase happen instead of outright refusing the voice's request, sleep would come much quicker. He could eventually drift off into a deep sleep barely hearing the alarm the next morning.

On several evenings he found himself sitting in his home office crunching numbers furiously on his calculator. A pencil scribbled on the notepad to his left. There might be a way to purchase the property without tapping too deeply into the retirement savings if he could sell some of the heifers off at a decent price. No. That wouldn't work. It was still too early in the year and they were still nursing the calves they'd dropped a few months earlier. The calves wouldn't be ready for market until the middle of fall. Perhaps if he sold a few acres of their farm to buy the new place? No. Myrna wouldn't be too happy about that. She loved this place as much as he did. It was their home. It was their lifelong dream. Later on when he drifted off to sleep, his dreams would be filled with numbers and possibilities, each one as farfetched and fanciful as the one before. There simply was no way around it. To purchase Johnson's place, they would either have to tap into their retirement savings or consider selling off some of their land.

He realized one afternoon as he picked the ears of Silver Queen that he had already made his decision. He was going to buy Johnson's land. He still didn't particularly want it. He had no idea what he would actually do with it other than go fishing on occasion, but he had to buy it. The mere notion had become an obsession for him. Now, his biggest obstacle sat shelling peas in the den.

Myrna was not keen on the idea in the slightest. She'd more than brought that point home the day he first mentioned it. He'd waited more than three weeks before bringing it up again, until the dreams and nightmares drove him once again to distraction. Again she firmly put her foot down. She didn't want Johnson's land. She had no need for that piece of property and she didn't want to be stuck with a large tax bill from the county for property she didn't want or need. They were all valid points but all completely irrelevant to his overwhelming and completely unexplainable need to purchase that land.

He loaded the buckets of corn into the trailer that was attached to his small riding lawn mower. Then he grabbed another bucket and went to pick the tomatoes and cucumbers. Maybe he could bring the topic up again while they shelled peas this evening. It wouldn't be easy but he had to convince her that they needed to buy this property. It was the only way he could ever hope to have peace of mind again.

"Well, let's see what exciting things we can find on TV tonight." Jimmy picked up his latest copy of Orbit magazine and began to scan the local listings.

"The African Queen is coming on. You want to watch that?"He peered to his left at Myrna who had just sat down with a fresh pan of peas to shell.

15

"That sounds good. We haven't seen that in a long time."

Jimmy went outside to adjust the satellite dish. The most prominent feature in their yard, many of his neighbors were more than a little puzzled when the Watson's constructed what appeared to be a NASA satellite dish beside their carport. It was quite the monstrosity. Over twenty feet wide, it had been a worthwhile investment when they first moved out to the country in the early '80s and could only get two of the three local channels on TV. Even with the monthly subscription rate which limited the number of channels they once received, they got more channels than any of their relatives in the city who had cable. And some of the naysayers in the county had made similar investments after seeing the wide selection of programming that was actually available. Why, the movie they were going to watch tonight was coming in from one of the western feeds. Couldn't do that with cable.

Back in his leather recliner, he punched the numbers into the receiver that sat on a small shelf centered behind his and Myrna's chairs. Then, he went into the kitchen, grabbed a dishpan, and filled it with field peas that lay spread out on newspaper on the floor. He returned to the den in time to hear Bogie's stomach growl in front of two rather dour protestant missionaries.

"I don't think that cup of tea is going to do." Jimmy said, willing Hepburn to throw a steak or pork chop into the mix.

"No. He needs a sandwich or something." Myrna agreed.

They sat in silence from that point on, shelling peas, and watching the adventures of a mismatched couple on an old steam boat as it traveled through the depths of Africa. Only the occasional comment was made about the movie.

"She went and poured out all his gin."

"He done messed up thinking he was going to talk her out of the rapids."

"She broke the blade and wants him to fix it."

All said with a laugh. All said a hundred times before. Jimmy loved this movie. In fact, it was one of his favorite Bogie films. Partly because of the scenery, partly because of the adventurous story, but mainly for the comical aggravation Hepburn put Bogie through. Hepburn was a force to be reckoned with much like his Myrna although Myrna had never caused him that much grief. Of course, she'd never taken on the German Navy either, which was probably a good thing for the Germans.

The brown paper sack between them was full of hulls by the time the movie was over. It was still more than an hour before the late night news came on so Jimmy switched channels to a Braves game. It wasn't as entertaining as the movie. They were up five to nothing in the bottom of the fifth and looked to be playing a bunch of little leaguers. Jimmy went and reloaded his pan of peas and decided to once again broach the subject that was weighing heaviest on his mind.

"I know you don't want to do it, but I feel like we need to buy Johnson's old place."

"No, I don't." She retorted.

"I have to buy it."

"Jimmy, I thought we had already settled this. We don't need that land."

He nodded. "I know we don't need it. And I know we never wanted it, but I have to buy it. I can't explain why, but it's been worrying me to death ever since I saw Johnson's obituary in the paper. I can't sleep and I can't think about anything else."

She was not convinced. "Why do you have to have that property all of the sudden? Don't you have enough to take care of here?"

"I don't know why I have to buy it. I just do or won't have a minute's peace."

She continued to shell the peas as she thought for a few more moments. "Can you afford it with you being retired now?"

"Yeah, it'll make things a little tighter. But we should be okay."

Myrna looked at him for a little while longer. After all this time together she knew him better than anyone else in the world, but this was a new one. She'd known him to have sleepless nights before, especially when business was particularly tough. But this? This was not like him at all.

"Well, if it's worrying you that bad, then we better buy it. I don't know why you want it so bad or what we'll do with it but it ain't worth cracking up over."

He smiled when he heard the straightforward response he'd expected. "Yeah, that's kinda what I thought too."

Chapter Two

"HEY THERE, JIMMY. How are you doing, old man?" Bill answered the phone with a familiar greeting to his friend.

"Getting older by the minute, it feels like." Jimmy smiled in spite of himself.

"It's a good thing we were both born pretty." Bill laughed.

"Yeah, ain't that the truth!"

"Hadn't heard from you in awhile. What's going on?"

"Bill, I need you to do me a favor."

"Sure, man. What do you need?"

"I'm going to buy ol' man Johnson's place. I want you to get things going for me." He listened for Bill's jaw to drop on the other end.

"That old hermit who died?"

"Yep. That's the one." Jimmy stated matter-of-factly.

"What in the world do you want to buy that old rundown place for?"

"Well, I heard that guy Trump talking about making millions of dollars in real estate. Thought this could be my big break." He smiled to himself.

"You're kidding!"

"You gotta start somewhere, Bill."

"Well, look Jim, if you want to start looking at investment properties, I got about twenty here that'd be better than that old place."

"Gotta be that one, Bill."

"What do you mean it's got to be that one?"

"That's the one I want."

Bill took a deep breath. "May I ask you why you woke up all of the sudden wanting the most worthless piece of property in the county that isn't even on the market yet?" He sincerely hoped his friend was pulling his leg although Jimmy had never taken anything to this level before.

"I can't really explain it, but I have to buy it and it has to be that piece of property."

"Have you been drinking?" It was a long shot but he had to make sure.

"Bill, you know I don't drink."

"I know, but that was the only thing that might make sense of this crazy conversation."

"I can't make sense of it. I just know I have to buy that property."

"And you're not going to tell me why?"

"I can't explain it."

He took another deep breath. "Jim, I've known you all my life and this is the most harebrained idea you've ever come up with."

"Yeah it is."

"But you want me to do it?"

"Yeah, I do."

"Alright, I'll start working on it for you."

"Thanks Bill."

CB&O

Jimmy crossed the railroad tracks on his way to old man Johnson's farm. He'd never actually walked the property before. He only saw it in his dreams. Now that he'd started the wheels turning on the possible purchase, he wanted to know what he was actually in for. He steered his Ford pickup past the old general store onto the dirt road that ran along the railroad tracks. He knew some of the neighbors had mentioned to the county that it needed to be paved to prevent the dirt from washing so badly but Johnson had raised a fuss and the issue died before it ever really got started.

He parked beside the old 'A' frame home. The siding had seen better days. That would need to be repaired. So would the roof. Shingles were missing in several spots. It would be a wonder if the whole house wasn't full of mildew. He made a mental note to check the sheetrock for signs of damage. He was certain they wouldn't be hard to spot. He checked along the outside of the window ledges. They would have to be replaced as well. The paint on the home peeled off ages ago and had never been reapplied. The wood was rotten in several places along each ledge. The house was standing but in desperate need of attention. Fortunately, he didn't see any outward signs of serious structural damage but he would need to further exam that once he walked around inside.

Behind the house stood a small storage shed. It was leaning at an awkward angle and would probably come down after he'd finished with fixing up the house. For now, it would be a good place to store any tools or equipment that he might need for the renovation. Nothing overly valuable of course, (a child could have broken through that door with a slingshot) but things that he didn't want to get wet or damaged from the weather. All in all, it might not be as bad as he'd originally feared.

The property stretched for about fifteen acres through the woods. He had already gone to the county office and gotten a copy of the plat so that he had a rough idea of the boundaries. He gathered the diagram from his truck and set off on foot to survey his potential purchase. The property was in an odd triangle formation with a very narrow easement to the main road. He thought about subdividing the property into lots but that would require an additional purchase of land on either side to build an access road. He needed to talk to Bill about that and see if either owner would be willing to sell a few acres.

He traced the property up an embankment and along a thoroughly overgrown field. The tree growth indicated that nothing had been grown here for at least ten years. The baby long leaf pines were well on their way toward maturity and already up to about three feet tall. It wouldn't be difficult to clear this land and section off lots. There were a few pin oaks that would offer good shade. He would leave as many of those in place as he could when dividing the land. People always wanted mature trees on a property. Those should help the lots sell more quickly. Meandering around, he came to a thicket of woods and the remains of an old brick fireplace. This must be the remnants of the home that was listed on the plat from the 1930's. Nothing remained of the home today except for a four foot high soot covered section of chimney. Perhaps a fire had brought the home crashing down. It was difficult to tell now but he would look into it further.

A little way away from the chimney stood a mighty mulberry tree towering over all around her. Jimmy could tell she was far older than any of the other vegetation around. Perhaps as much as a hundred years old but that was just guessing. There was no way to know for sure. Standing beneath its shade brought to mind another day long ago. He took a picture from his wallet and smiled. This tree was a good sign. Everything was going to work out for the best.

CঞৎৡO

Johnson's estate seemed to be as disheveled and unwelcoming as his life had been. His only daughter, Terry Zucker, who now resided in California, flew in for the funeral, such as it was, and promptly set about collecting anything of value, a few pieces of jewelry that once belonged to her mother, a photo of her grandmother, any cash that happened to be hidden in sock drawers or behind the dresser mirror. She seemed to know most if not all of her father's secret hiding places. She was much less concerned with the man himself. They had fallen out years before and no amount of reconciliation could have mended that broken fence, not that either of them tried to restore any hard feelings. They had drifted apart and as a result now lived as far removed from one another as it was physically possible to do within the continental United States.

The idea of wasting precious time sorting out the estate of a man she regarded with such contempt held little interest to her, except for the property. That little piece of land might be the solution to her current financial difficulties. Jobs could be hard to come by for someone with such a sensitive immune system. Some bosses didn't understand the difficulties she faced on a daily basis. So when she received a call from Bill Dunne regarding a possible interested party for the land, she wasted no time in setting the transaction in motion. Prices had to be negotiated, of course. The offer was terribly low. In many ways, Georgia was still back in the stone ages with their property values, but that could be worked out to something more satisfactory. Maybe the death of her estranged father had a benefit after all.

CRED

"Hey, Mama." Robby called as he opened the sliding glass door on the back porch. His two sons, Jake and Heath, followed closely behind him.

Myrna looked up from the stove. Those boys were shooting up faster than anything. They were both as tall as their father and would soon dwarf him if they didn't stop growing. She hugged them both in turn before embracing her son. "Hey. I didn't know y'all were coming over today. Where's Laura and Abby?"

"Laura decided that they needed a girl's day out so she took them both shopping." Robby replied with a shrug. "We came over here to see about some of the scrap pieces of wood Dad has down at the barn. The boys wanted to make Laura a piece of furniture for her birthday."

"Oh, that'll be nice." Myrna approved.

"Yeah, Mr. Hayes said we can make whatever we want in class as long as we bring in the wood and supplies to do it. We figured Grandpa had plenty of pieces that would make something nice." Heath explained.

"Is he your wood shop teacher?"

"Yes, ma'am." Jake chimed in. "I have him for first period and then Heath takes his class after lunch. We should be able to finish it in half the time as everybody else."

"Well, that's a good thing. Her birthday is next month." Myrna reminded them.

Robby laughed. "There's no use getting in a rush about things, Mom."

Myrna shot him a look as she stirred the peas. "I guess not."

She continued to work on lunch as the boys talked about the grand plan for a new bookcase for their mom's bedroom. It would be a barrister style case with the pull down glass doors. They had seen a picture in one of the shop magazines at school and Mr. Hayes said he would give them extra credit if they completed the project before the end of this term. They were going to finish it in a cherry stain to match the bedroom furniture. They couldn't wait to see her face when they gave it to her. She was always saying she needed more space for her books.

"She'll really like that a lot." Myrna agreed. "Get some plates and go set the table."

"Hey Robby," Jimmy said, greeting his oldest son.

"Hey Dad. Been working in the garden?"

"Trying to get the peanuts in the ground." Jimmy confirmed.

"Good. Gotta have peanuts for football season."

"If they all make, then we'll have plenty."

Jimmy went to wash up while Myrna finished getting the meal on the table. The boys poured tea for everyone except Myrna who staunchly drank water. Once the tomatoes and cucumbers were sliced, it was time to eat. Not as big of a meal as they normally ate in the evening but more than enough to quench everyone's appetite. During lunch, the boys filled their grandpa in on their furniture making plans.

"There's plenty of wood down there. Go on down and help yourself."

Robby stayed behind while the boys went to explore in the barn. He'd go down in a bit to make sure they picked pieces that would work well, but for now there was no rush.

"I've got something I'm going to want you to take a look at sometime in the next couple of weeks." Jimmy opened up the conversation.

"What's that?" Robby helped himself to the rest of the tomatoes before his mother could tell him to finish them off.

"I'm going to buy old man Johnson's place and I want you to take a look at the house."

"You're going to buy another house?" Robby wanted to make sure he heard correctly.

"Yeah. Bill is working it up now."

"Why?"

"I just need to buy it." Jimmy was firm but unforthcoming.

"Do you want it?" He stared at his father.

"Not really."

The silence from Myrna was deafening.

"If you don't really want it, then why are you buying it?" Robby had worked with his father in the family business before his father retired and now owned his own small construction business. They usually shared most of their business ideas. This was something completely new and unheard of.

"It's worrying me to death. I have to buy it."

Myrna began clearing the dishes away but still remained silent on the issue. Somehow, Robby found her voice to be the loudest in the room. He looked to his mother, then at his father unsure of which side to take in the underlying debate.

"Well, just let me know what day you want me to look at it." He said as diplomatically as possible.

ය෴ඪ

31

"Did Dad talk to you about old man Johnson's place?" Robby watched his brother Dylan as he removed the carburetor from the '65 Mustang.

"No. What about it?" Dylan strained with a rusty bolt.

"He's planning on buying it."

"Buying what?" Dylan adjusted the wrench for a better grip.

"Old man Johnson's place." Robby reiterated.

Dylan twisted too hard causing the wrench to slip completely off the bolt. He rose up from the hood waving a bloody hand, grabbed a shop rag, and applied some pressure.

"Dad is going to buy what?"

Robby explained the conversation he'd had with their father over lunch. He also relayed their mother's frosty response.

"First I've heard about it." Dylan checked on his battered knuckle.

"Yeah, me too."

"And he didn't tell you why he had to buy it?" Dylan draped the rag across the grill.

"No. Just said it was worrying him to death."

"That's weird. Nothing ever worries Daddy."

CB&D

Bill unlocked the key box on the door for the men to enter. Jimmy, Robby, Dylan, and he all looked on with some trepidation as the list of repairs seemed to grow. Jimmy had seen several things that needed addressing when he walked the exterior of the property. Now seeing things from the inside, he saw his worse fears realized. All the appliances in the kitchen were prehistoric. He doubted if all the eyes on the stove actually worked. Several of the knobs were missing from the kitchen cabinets. Tile was missing in the home's only bathroom. Not only would repairs need to be made to that bath, he would also need to incorporate another bath into his remodeling plans to make the home sellable. The floor sagged in the living room area. It would need to be replaced. Once in the basement, he saw the reason for the sag. One of the support beams was rotten and giving way to the weight above. He would have to replace that first, then worry about the floor above.

Both Dylan and Robby scratched their heads at the whole thing. It would take a lot of work to be inhabitable. Heck, it'd take a lot of work to make it worth the expense of a wrecking ball.

"Dad, are you sure you want this old house?" Dylan looked at his father.

"Yeah. I'm sure."

"There are a lot of other houses that would make a good rental property investment. I'm sure Bill would be happy to show you some of those." Robby said hopefully.

"I've got a list of them in my office. We can look at them anytime." Bill confirmed.

"This is the property I need to buy." Jimmy was firm. They all knew the battle was lost.

ଓଞ୍ଚ

Shannon saw the email from her sister first thing that morning but didn't have a chance to open it until after lunch. The world had gone topsy-turvy. Everyone who normally acted rational was in a dither and those who usually panicked were calm. She couldn't make heads nor tails of the whole phenomenon other than perhaps she'd fallen in some sort of black hole and come out in a universe where nothing made sense. It was a mystery. Every client had a problem that demanded immediate attention and every employee was at a loss for a solution.

Now, as she sat nibbling on the last few chips she'd packed for her lunch, she opened the email from her sister. It had been over two weeks since they'd spoken. Emma was probably checking in to see how things were going.

> *To:*
> *<SGranger@stewartmanufactoring.net>*
> *From: <emmaandjoe7475@gmail.com>*
> *Subject: Hey*
>
> *Hey sis! Just wanted to send you a quick note to see if you'd talked to mom and dad recently. Robby said they were planning on buying old man Johnson's place. Have you heard anything about it? Hope you and the kids are good. Love ya chica!*

Old man Johnson's place? What? Shannon wracked her brain to try to remember exactly who old man Johnson was and where he lived. She couldn't place the name or a face which was unusual in such a small community. Great! Now her family had gone crazy too. Suddenly a cabin in the mountains sounded better and better.

Myrna answered the phone a few minutes later.

"Hey, Mama. Are you guys moving?"

"No."

"Emma sent me an email today. She said you guys were buying another farm?" Shannon was still confused.

"Your Daddy is going to buy Johnson's old place."

Again Shannon searched her brain for any hint of Johnson. Having lived in North Atlanta for the last fifteen years had driven a few of the supporting characters from back home out of her mind. She couldn't quite picture his face or where he lived.

"Johnson who?"

Shannon listened as her mom explained about the old hermit who lived beside the railroad tracks. Of course she remembered where it was, you entered the place at the old general store. And she probably didn't remember Johnson because the old hermit never ventured out much by the time she was in high school. Shannon began to piece together the location but not the reasoning.

"So, y'all aren't moving?"

"No, I'm not moving over there." Myrna wouldn't entertain such an idea.

"So what's dad planning on doing with it?"

"He doesn't know yet. Maybe subdivide." Myrna stated with a huff.

"Well, that sounds like a good investment then. There should be a lot of prospective buyers especially with the expansion at the base."

"That's what he thinks."

"Oh, okay. Daddy always was one to find a good investment."

"We'll see how good it is." Myrna was resigned to the idea if still not particularly happy about it.

Shannon wasn't sure what the fuss was about but she knew she'd hear something about it on her next trip home. At least now she could go back to fixing all the problems that fell on her desk this morning.

CR80

Bill read the letter from Terry Zucker twice. She was definitely interested in selling the property but her prices were well above the market value for this area. He'd only spoken to her once when he initially called to convey his client's interest in the property. She had responded favorably until he told her what the average price per acre was locally. She hadn't exactly scoffed, but her voice dripped with disappointment. Now he saw why. She had an overinflated idea of the worth of that little piece of land.

He picked up the phone and dialed the number listed on the letter. It was midweek and there was a good possibility that she would be at work, especially at this time of the day. On the second ring she answered.

"Hello, Ms. Zucker. This is Bill Dunne. We spoke on the phone last week."

"Oh, yes, Mr. Dunne." This was the call she'd been waiting for. "How are you?"

"I'm doing good, thank you. How are you today?"

"Absolutely wonderful." Any hint that she'd once had a Southern drawl was long since gone.

"That's good to hear."

"So what can I do for you today, Mr. Dunne? Did you get my letter?" She knew there was no other reason for him to call other than to discuss the sale of her father's property. The sooner she could unload it, the better off she'd be.

"Yes, ma'am. I did get that." He paused for a moment while he put on his reading glasses. "As a matter of fact, that's what I'd like to talk to you about."

"Fire away, Mr. Dunne."

"I see that the price you'd like to get for the property is well over double the estimated value. I don't think realistically you'll ever come close to that amount of money."

Silence.

"Ms. Zucker, are you there?" He thought for a moment the line had gone dead.

"Yes, I'm here." Her voice had suddenly developed a steely tone.

"Okay, thought for a minute I had lost you. Did you hear what I was saying about the asking price?" Bill felt an unexpected chill run down his spine. This lady was her father in a dress.

"Yes. I heard that. I must say that's rather disappointing."

"I'm sure it is, Ms. Zucker. But in all honesty, I don't think that land will even fetch the average price per acre because of where it's located. You have to remember, it's almost completely landlocked. Only a small access drive goes in or out. There's really nothing anyone could do with that land. It's not even good farm land."

Her nostrils flared a bit at that. It was her land now and she never owned anything that was subpar. "I have many fond memories of that land, Mr. Dunne. I assure you it is quite valuable to me."

"I have no doubt. That's where you grew up and we always place a high value on our home." Bill tried to smooth things over. He was trying to remember if he'd ever heard of her coming back to visit her father in all the years she'd been away but decided not to venture down that road.

She took a long drag on her cigarette. "What exactly are you suggesting?"

"I've spoken to my client and he is prepared to make an offer on that property. A fair offer at that. I'd like to send it over to you. You're free to negotiate the price as you see fit, but I can honestly say, my client will not be willing to pay the price you listed in your letter. No one in this area will pay that. You'd be sitting on that land for many years to come at that price."

"When are you sending over the offer?"

He could hear the ice clinking in the glass at the other end of the phone and only imagined what indulgences she was enjoying at this time of day.

"Do you have a fax machine? If so, I can send it over to you in the next hour or so. If not, I'll put it in an overnight envelope."

There was no fax machine. Who did he think she was, anyway? She lived in a nice home not an office complex with computers and printers whirring about. She'd look the offer over once it arrived. Half the price she wanted. It was an outrage. She wouldn't stand for it one minute. This client of his would simply have to pay more. That was all there was to be said in the matter. Half the price would greatly cut into her long term plans.

She wondered if Dunne had been correct. Would the client walk away if the price was too high? Those people back home could be stubborn at times. She wouldn't put it past the old coot to try to talk the client out of buying the property to begin with. He probably thought he was some big shot, some real estate mogul. She'd show him. He didn't know who he was dealing with.

Bill stared at the phone for a few minutes before he thought about calling Jimmy. That woman would be a pistol ball to deal with. She had the idea she was sitting on a gold mine when it was really a bunch of pyrite. Now he had to make sure his friend really wanted to go through with this headache and discuss the offer price he'd just implied he already had. He doubted she'd come down off her pedestal, but he'd make the offer like Jimmy wanted. What else are friends for but to jump in a hornet's nests together?

CB&O

She stared at the pile of bills on the table, then back at the paltry offer Dunne had sent her. He'd broken it down for her so she could see the purchase price for the house and the land. Dunne actually thought the land was more valuable than the house. That house would fetch ten times the offer if it was here in California. She looked at the deadline for response. She had to make a decision today or the offer would be void. There was no guarantee that she'd get another one and if so, it might be less than this.

Still, she was unsure. She added up the bills again. If she took the offer, she could pay off all her bills but wouldn't be able to buy the new car she wanted. If she didn't take it, she didn't know when she could climb out from under this mountain. She really needed a car. Hers was limping along ready to die. Perhaps if she sent back a counteroffer that raised the purchase price enough to cover the expense of a car, she could get rid of this headache and meet the needs she had. It was a risk but one she felt she had to take. Her ex-husband had always told her to never accept the first offer. Always come back with a counter. It was all part of the negotiation dance as he called it. He was a putz but he knew how to swing a big deal. She would take his advice one last time.

She called Bill to let him know she was sending back a counteroffer for the client. He would get it first thing Monday morning. Thus began her excruciating waiting game. She never liked haggling over the price of anything. But this was haggling on a much grander scale, one which she was unfamiliar with. She had to keep her wits about her if she hoped to close the deal quickly.

When the call came through Tuesday, she feared the worst. Mr. Dunne reviewed the proposal and stated that they would send back a revised offer. More than the original but much lower than she wanted. The intercontinental bidding war was on. After two weeks of this, the bills on her kitchen table had become unmanageable. The harassing phone calls of bill collectors barraged her hourly. It was more than she could bear. And still the latest offer would not allow for the purchase of a new car. She looked at the offer as the phone rang from an unidentified number. Another creditor demanding money she didn't have. Didn't they know she had difficulty working a steady job? She waited for the call to go to the answering machine and dialed Mr. Dunne's number. She would take the offer. She had little choice at this point. At least it would solve some of her problems and it would finally rid her of the final ties to a miserable past. Nothing but bright lights ahead, once she paid a few things off. All she needed was another chance at a fresh start.

◌ॐ◌

"Well, looks like you got your wish." Bill greeted as his friend answered the phone.

"She agreed?"

"Yeah. I still think it's a bit too high. I'm sure if we held out a little longer we could have gotten her to come down a bit but, she called just now to let me know she had accepted the offer and will be sending back the signed agreement. Once I get that back, I type up a clean copy for us all to keep in our records and schedule the closing."

"Thanks, Bill. I appreciate it."

They closed on the land five weeks later. Terry had to make arrangements to travel back to Georgia for the closing as well as getting all the items out of the house. She had no idea what she would do with all that junk. She didn't need the furniture but maybe she could hold some sort of garage sale and get rid of a lot of it. The new owner, a Mr. Jimmy Watson whom she couldn't remember from her time growing up had offered to give her an extra month to clear out. Dunne said there was normally a fee for that but Watson hadn't charged anything saying that it was a difficult situation all the way around with her being clear on the other side of the country and all. It was the least he could do since the two of them had practically robbed her of her father's land but she would make every effort to be civil while she was there. No use in upsetting someone who was trying to be nice, even if the niceness was because of guilt.

Chapter Three

THE HOUSE WAS every bit as bad as Jimmy had suspected. He began by replacing the roof and all the fascia boards around the eaves. They'd rotted clear through. He was lucky that none of the rafters needed replacing. Only some of the plywood along the edges where the fascia boards had caused sagging and warping were replaced. It had taken him almost a week to finish that part of the job. Robby and Dylan both helped when they could but with both of his boys running their own businesses, there was only so much they could get to during the week.

Terry Zucker still had quite a bit of stuff stored the house. She was what Bill called a 'character.' His friend used that term to describe a plethora of people from the funny to the frazzled and those who fell somewhere in between. Terry was in her own category of 'character.' He suspected she probably fit in well with some of the more questionable characters out in California although he ventured that even they might be ready to send her back. He understood it was difficult to travel coast to coast on a regular basis, but he'd hoped that she would have finished moving most of the stuff out before she went back after the closing. Apparently, something important had come up and she simply couldn't work on clearing out her father's items. She skipped out of the attorney's office holding the certified check and promised to return within two weeks. That was six weeks ago.

He'd put off working on any major projects around the house until she got her stuff out, but with the weather turning colder, he didn't want to wait on some of the repairs and risk causing major water damage. He was glad he had gone ahead and started. That roof wouldn't survive another good storm. It was a miracle it had survived this long. Next he planned on replacing the windows and the window seals. Then he really needed to get started on the inside. He only hoped she would come and get her stuff by then.

A month later, she still had not returned and his patience was wearing thin. He had already sent her several letters, all of which went unanswered. He had little choice but to contact the sheriff. There would be a thirty day waiting period, but the county would notify her that her property would be evicted from the premises unless she came and got it immediately. A few nights later, Jimmy answered the phone for the first of several drunken rants. Terry was not a woman to be toyed with by some hick town nobody. She had powerful friends and wasn't afraid to call on them in a moment's notice.

"Do you have any friends over here?" Jimmy asked with far less patience than usual.

"I haf frands everwhere!" She stammered.

"Well, that's good. Send them over to the house this week and get your stuff."

She slammed the phone down and didn't call back for several more days. When he heard from her again, she was completely sober and back to the stilted charm she tried desperately to master.

"Good afternoon, Mr. Watson. I do hope I haven't interrupted you from anything important." She offered a flirty laugh.

"No. Nothing important." He had just finished chopping a cord of wood for the winter when the rain started and forced him inside.

"Oh, that's good." She gushed. "I was hoping to talk to you about this unfortunate matter about the property in the house."

"I was wondering when you wanted to come and get it."

"You see that's the problem. I simply can't come over there before this nasty business with the sheriff expires. Is there any way to get an extension?" he could tell she was a woman who was used to using her assets rather than her intelligence and fortitude to get what she wanted.

"I'm afraid I can't extend it any longer." Jimmy was firm.

"And may I ask why not?" The crack in her armor was almost unperceivable.

"It's already been three months and I really need to get working on the inside of that house. I don't want to do anything while your stuff is still inside."

She resumed her previous tactic. "I know it's been inconvenient for you but I truly can't get over there at the moment. My funds are all tied up. I have no way to travel."

"I'm sorry to hear that."

"So you'll reconsider?" She had him now.

"No. No, I'm afraid I can't push it back any further."

"I would have thought a man claiming to have Christian charity would be willing to work with someone who was down and out." The claws came out.

"I'm sorry you find yourself in a financial bind but if the money was going to be a problem then you should have stayed when you were over here the last time and worked on getting your stuff out. I haven't charged you a single dime but I need that stuff out of the house."

"Fine! Do whatever you want to with it. Give it to Goodwill. Throw it away. I don't care but I'm not coming back." She bellowed.

"If that's what you want me to do, then send me something in writing stating that fact. Otherwise, I'm not going to touch it without the sheriff."

It was the last time they ever spoke. A few days later a letter arrived stating in no uncertain terms that she would not be returning and he was to remove the contents of the house at his convenience. He could dispose of them as he saw fit. At least it was a solution but not the one he had hoped for. Moving someone else's things out of the old house added several weeks of aggravation to his already limited patience where this house was concerned. Perhaps everyone around him was right and he shouldn't have bought this property. Logically, he knew that was the case, but somewhere deep inside a calm settled. He still believed this was the right decision.

⋆⋆⋆

Jimmy leaned over the dining room table with his eldest son staring at a copy of the plat. They needed to find the best way to bring a road through to maximize the number and size of the lots to be sold while still leaving adequate access to the renovated house.

"We should probably run the road up through this way and circle it around here." Robby ran his finger over the map to show his father where he felt the road should go.

Jimmy studied this for a moment. Robby's idea would take the road through the old ruined chimney and possibly take out much of that area. He suggested an alternate path.

"But you'd lose at least one lot going that way." Robby countered.

"True, but this area here has a major drop off. We wouldn't be able to get the lots you said without some serious work. This way we can still have a reasonable number of lots for sale without as much prep work.

Robby was unconvinced. Prep work wouldn't be that difficult. They already had the equipment. It was just a matter of knocking over a few trees and leveling out some of the dirt.

"No. I think we're going to go up this way." Jimmy took a pencil and lightly drew in the line for the proposed road, completely avoiding any potential damage to the old chimney and the trees around it.

Robby couldn't understand it. This was the second time in recent months when his dad had made a decision that seemed out of character. But, once the pencil mark had been drawn, there was no going back. For Dad, it was etched in stone. Now, the real fun began. Permits would have to be acquired. The surveyor would have to be scheduled. New plans would need approval. The county would have final say of course, but they didn't foresee any major complications with the process. They'd both worked through the system numerous times before. It would be time consuming and a bit costly, but if it was done right the first time, which Jimmy was a stickler for, the project should flow smoothly.

∞

He put the third box of old photos, trinkets, letters, and odd pieces of jewelry in the spare bedroom. The letter had said she was not in the position to return and collect her things from the house. He could dispose of them any way he wanted. Most of the larger items of furniture and clothes had already been donated to a local shelter for battered women. They were always in need of items to help families start again. Some of the items such as books and whatnots had gone to Goodwill. These were all that was left of Terry Zucker's birth family. Three boxes of mementos. Somehow he couldn't bring himself to throw them away despite everything. He knew if it had been his family he would have wanted to keep them. He reached in his pocket and pulled out the envelope that he'd used to stuff the miscellaneous stashes of cash he'd found. He was honestly surprised that she hadn't come across these as she hastily searched. It was obvious that the money was all that held her attention. She must have truly hated the old man to overlook more than a thousand dollars in cold hard cash.

Legally, all these items were his. He could toss them and use the cash to fix up the house in desperate need of repair. Morally, he felt a different pull. He made his way to his office, took out a legal pad, and began to write.

Dear Ms. Zucker,

I found these items along with $1,037 in cash that I feel should be returned to you. As your letter states, I can dispose of the items as I wish. Therefore, I am putting three boxes in the mail today with your parent's personal effects. I'll use the cash I found for the postage and send you the remaining amount in the form of a Postal Money Order.

Regards,
Jimmy Watson

That would settle his accounts with her and with his conscience.

ଓଞ୍ଚ

The surveyor was in a similar agreement with Robby. They could definitely get more lots in the area if the road went near the old chimney. They would have to take out all the trees in the area, but it could be done. When Jimmy refused to budge on the idea, he simply shrugged and went about the business of marking off the individual lots as requested. Flags and markers were put out to indicate where the road would go. The county inspectors agreed to the plan and issued the necessary permits.

Finding a good paving company was slightly more complicated. Jimmy had always worked with Forsyth Paving in the past. He had known Chuck Forsyth for years and knew any project Chuck worked on would be done right. Jimmy called to schedule a time for Chuck to come out and look at things but was informed it would be well after New Year's before they could even think about looking at it. Chuck had landed several large development projects in Atlanta that would take at least six weeks to complete. With the holidays coming up, that would push things back to the first or second week of January.

Jimmy didn't like the idea of pushing things back that far. He decided to call around to see which other companies were available. Three different companies came out and estimated the job. Each was cheaper than Chuck would have been. Two were considerably cheaper. Saving money was good, but they seemed too cheap. He knew from experience that a road that isn't paved correctly is nothing but a headache. He would never get an inadequate road approved by the county nor would he have any hopes of selling the lots if potential buyers saw sloppy pavement. These guys were new to the business and although they seemed professional, he decided to go where experience led him. He called Chuck and scheduled an appointment for the second week of January.

CЗ&O

"So, what are you getting Mom and Dad for Christmas?" Shannon asked her older sister.

"I don't know. What are you getting them?" Emma replied.

It was the same conversation they'd had every year since they were teens. The first week of December began with a frantic search to find presents for the only two people on Earth who wanted absolutely nothing. Neither of their parents were gadgety people so they had no interest in the latest gizmos. Both liked to read but you'd be hard pressed to find the right book for either of them since both were particular about their reading choices. Knick-knacks already lined the shelves from Christmases and anniversaries past when no other suitable gift could be found. Dad had spent the last forty years amassing every tool known to man. Mom had more kitchenware than she would ever use. She didn't like candles or perfumes. He never wore ties. It was a mystery.

"Do you think Mom would like jewelry?" Shannon offered.

"Dad always gets Mom a bracelet for Christmas." Emma reminded her.

They both know their mother only wore jewelry on very special occasions. There was a long pause.

"What about a dessert cookbook? You know Mom loves to bake." Emma offered.

"That's a good idea for you, but now what am I going to get her? And Dad? What in the world can we get him?" Shannon dreaded the idea of wandering aimlessly through Wal-Mart in a quest to find some unknown gift. She knew she had to have some kind of game plan before she left for the store.

"Dad needs some new slippers." Emma said triumphantly.

"Slippers?"

"And maybe some new socks." Emma was on a roll now.

"Slippers and socks?" Shannon rolled her eyes. "That's the best you can do?"

"Well, what else do you want to get him?" Emma retorted.

"I don't know but I was hoping for something a little more substantial than socks and slippers." Shannon could just picture the mobs of people fighting down each aisle, everyone as lost as she would be.

"Fine, then I'll get them for him."

"No! You're getting Mom the cookbook. I still don't have anything for her." Shannon was not going to lose out on both ideas.

"But they were both my ideas."

Once again, her sister had completely missed the point of this conversation. "We're trying to come up with ideas mutually."

Emma was unconvinced. "Then what are your ideas?"

"It's called brainstorming. It's not about individual success. It's about coming up with ideas together so that we each have a halfway decent gift for our parents."

"Hmph." Emma snorted. "Next year we should probably start brainstorming in January."

"Yeah. That's what we said last year."

They dissolved into a fit of laughter knowing that they each would need to race to the store to be the first to buy Dad a new pair of slippers.

ം

Jimmy was caulking the windows in the living room when the electrician showed up.

"Boy, Wilbur, am I glad to see you." Jimmy greeted and offered a handshake.

"This place is a little hard to find. Drove by here twice." Wilbur replied.

"Yeah, once we get the road paved, we're going to replace the street sign."

Wilbur looked around at his friend's latest project. "Looks like you found yourself a real fixer upper."

"Yep." Jimmy reluctantly agreed.

"So what's this problem you're having with an outlet?"

"I'm afraid it might be more than the outlet." Jimmy recounted how the day before he had plugged the miter saw into the kitchen outlet. Before he could finish with the first cut, the outlet blew. He unplugged the saw and made sure there were no other electronic devises plugged in but he needed to be sure that the house wouldn't go up in an electrical fire.

Wilbur looked at the charred cover of the outlet and the singe marks along the wall. "Hmmm. That is a bad sign right there, Jimmy."

"Yep." Jimmy nodded in agreement.

Jimmy showed Wilbur where the electrical box was and then left to go and finish the caulking. Each window in the house had been replaced. Now the caulk would keep any drafts from seeping around the edges. He was finishing up the ones in the master bedroom when Wilbur gave him the bad news. The wiring wasn't up to code. It would need to be replaced. There were no circuit interrupter outlets as required by code. Those would need to be installed. The breaker box had been installed as an afterthought, probably to replace an older fuse box. Half the wires aren't even connected. There was no rhyme or reason to the whole thing.

"All I can say is whoever wired this house before was an idiot." Wilbur affirmed.

"Yeah, that's what I was afraid of." Jimmy nodded.

"Honestly, the whole thing needs to be redone."

"Hmmm." Even though it was expected, that was not the news Jimmy wanted to hear.

"What do you want me to do?" Wilbur asked.

"Well, I can't have a house without electricity and I can't have a house that doesn't meet code. It's gotta be fixed."

"Alright, let me go back to my shop and get some more supplies that I'll need. I'll be back with a couple of guys this afternoon to get started."

"Okay." Jimmy agreed. He made a mental note to call his HVAC guy after Wilbur finished to check that system out. It would probably need to be replaced as well. Then he remembered he hadn't noticed a problem with the plumbing yet. Better schedule that appointment with the plumber ahead of time, just in case.

❧

Shannon was the last to arrive carrying a large casserole dish of homemade macaroni and cheese. It was her standard dish, homemade without complexity. The perfect dish for any family gathering. She placed it on the table between the sweet potatoes and the ham before offering those around her a Christmas hug.

"Where are the kids?" Myrna asked.

"They're in there under the tree trying to figure out which present is theirs." Shannon smiled.

"They won't have to wait long. Dinner is almost ready. Just have to pull the rolls out of the oven."

The wait, as it happened, was insurmountable to the youngsters. Why did it always take adults so long to eat? And what was so important to talk about? Couldn't they talk after the presents? Even the teenagers seemed less interested in the presents than they should have been. Finally, everyone was gathered in the living room. Extra chairs had been brought in from the dining room and the kitchen tables. The younger kids sat on the floor. It was their job to hand out the gifts. Saved the old knees they were told. It also sped up the process considerably since adults never seemed to be in much of a hurry on Christmas. Wrapping paper began to litter the floor in reckless abandon. Myrna loved the cookbook from Emma. Jimmy liked the slippers from Shannon. Robby and Dylan both liked the new tool set they got from their parents. The kids were far too busy with cars and dolls to notice anything else.

Myrna watched as her living room carpet disappeared into a sea of color. It was good to have everyone together for Christmas. It was so rare that all the kids and grandkids met in one place at one time. Everybody was so busy with work and school. Robby's boys looked just like he did at their age. Jake and Heath were growing up so fast. Their sister Abby was an exact duplicate of their mother Laura. An x-ray tech at the hospital in Macon, she was the only one absent from the feast today. No rest for those in the medical field. Sickness never takes a holiday. Emma and Joel had their own brood forming. She had walked into a readymade family when she married him. Two little girls, Samantha and Christina, had been left motherless after a terrible traffic accident.

Poor dears were only toddlers at the time. Now, they were as much her children as the twin boys, Wayne and James, who at five years old were quite the pair of stinkers. Dylan and his wife Amy had the youngest child in the family. Little Tyler was almost two and giving his big sister Anna all the excitement she could handle. Anna and Katie, Shannon and Darren's daughter, were both three and far too sophisticated to deal with Tyler's antics. They retreated to their own separate corner with Samantha and Christina to play with their dolls without the aggravation of the boys who were actively trying to crash their new Hot Wheels. As Myrna looked out, it was hard to believe that she had ten grandchildren all gathered around the Christmas tree.

∞

Chuck Forsyth planned on paving the road the week following his initial visit but weather pushed that date back further. It was turning out to be one of the wettest and coldest winters on record. That was a good sign for farmers in the area but not so good for anyone trying to do outdoor construction. It was the first full week of February before the areas could be leveled off and the pavers could finally make an appearance.

The new furnace was working fine now that the house actually had some electricity flowing the way it was supposed to. Jimmy was able to work inside comfortably. The fresh paint that coated the walls added a sense of warmth to the former harsh white décor. Bill had been correct. Go with a neutral color. It would attract more buyers. Now the only major thing left was the flooring. The carpet was tattered and torn in many places. It simply had to go.

Robby and Dylan dragged the last of the old carpet out to the dumpster. Dad had found real hardwood underneath the forty year old fibers. So far it had been the best thing about Johnson's old home. Every other discovery had presented a new and time consuming challenge. The drywall in over half of the home had some sort of decay or mold issue. That had all been replaced. New crown molding was installed. Now, the home was almost finished and ready to be put on the market. Hardwoods would definitely add to the value of the place. Once all the carpeting was discarded, they would bring in the sanders and get to work prepping the floor for the stain and varnish. They had decided on a golden oak finish. It should complement the paint nicely. Then the last of the fixtures and lighting would be installed. Bill would have it officially listed before the end of the month. With the lots on the market, something should start to move before the end of spring. It would be good to recoup some of the investment.

It took Bill almost three months to find the right buyer. Tons of people walked through. Several people were interested. A few made an offer. They were willing to buy, if Jimmy would come down on the price. A lot. Jimmy knew the asking price was fair. Negotiations stalled and the house sat there unused and unloved.

Finally, they received an offer from the McIntyres. Joey and Linda McIntyre were an Air Force family on the cusp of retirement. They'd seen the world and now wanted to settle in a quiet area to raise their two children. This was the home they'd been looking for. Cozy with a large yard. Plenty of trees for privacy. Room for the kids to grow and play without the stresses of being cooped up in the city. They had actually looked at the home a month early when Bill was in the middle of negotiations with another couple, but they decided against putting in a bid at that time. They wanted to wait until Joey received word about the civilian job offer. The job came through and they were back to put pen to paper.

Jimmy looked at their offer. Lower than he wanted, but not insulting. Bill had been right. He could work with these people. After two weeks, they had a firm contract in hand. The final paperwork was signed three weeks later. The McIntyre's had their new home. Jimmy had one less headache to worry about. Now he could focus more attention on his garden and tending to his own house. He'd read an article in the Almanac about blacksmithing. There was a workshop up in the mountains next month. Perfect for beginners. They provided all the tools and equipment necessary. All he had to was show up for a few days. It was something he'd always wanted to try his hand at. There were all sorts of things you could make if you knew how to blacksmith. With this house off his hands, maybe he should take a few days off and learn the art of bending metal.

Chapter Four

JIMMY FIRST NOTICED the stitch in his side as he tilled up the garden. He must have slept wrong or pulled a muscle, although he didn't remember anything unusual. It was probably nothing. By noon, he realized it was definitely something. He could barely stand up straight as he walked up to the house and told his wife that he needed to see a doctor. Myrna didn't need to be told twice. Jimmy was not one who liked to waste time at the doctor's office. If he said he needed to go, he needed to go bad.

They waited in the emergency room for almost an hour before he was seen by a young resident. She was knowledgeable and very thorough, running a series of tests and x-rays before rendering a diagnosis of gallstones. They should dissolve on their own so immediate treatment was not necessary. He was given a prescription for ursodiol to assist with the breakdown and pain medication with instructions for a restrictive diet and follow up with his physician.

The next day they were back in the ER as the pain had reached excruciation. Jimmy and Myrna listened as a surgeon explained how gallstones could cause blockages in the digestive system. Since the pain was so severe, his recommendation was for Jimmy to undergo surgery to remove the gallbladder completely.

Shannon, Emma, and Dylan arrived within minutes of one another to find their mother sitting alone in the waiting room outside the surgical unit.

"Are they still prepping him or have they already wheeled him back?" Dylan said sitting down beside his mother and draping his arm loosely around her shoulders.

"They took him back just a few minutes ago." A tinge of worry peeked through Myrna's stoic armor.

"What happened?"Emma was emphatic. "I thought they said he'd be fine yesterday?"

"It kept getting worse today. Pain medicine wouldn't even touch it. We came up here and they've been running all sorts of tests all afternoon. They finally said he needed surgery." It had been a long day for Myrna.

"That pain must have been bad for Daddy to complain about it." Shannon acknowledged.

The others agreed. Their father was not one to give in to minor injuries. He'd worked construction for almost twenty years with a ruptured disc before finally having back surgery to repair it. His pain threshold was legendary.

"Well, the good news is gallbladder surgery is routine these days. He'll be sore for a little bit but he'll be fine. There's nothing to worry about." Dylan comforted Myrna as much as he could.

"Yeah, that's what the doctor said." Myrna agreed. They fell into an easy silence with Dylan rubbing his mom's shoulders while the girls flipped through some old magazines.

"Did you ever get in touch with Robby?" Emma asked.

Dylan nodded. "He'll be leaving first thing in the morning. Should get back sometime late tomorrow afternoon."

"I'm surprised he didn't leave when you called him." Emma wanted the whole family together. Hospitals made her anxious.

"It was storming there on the coast when I called. He didn't want to leave in that plus he'd only have about two hours of daylight on all those back roads. I told him to wait until the morning."

"There was no use in him leaving tonight. Don't want to risk him getting in a wreck when there's nothing he can do anyway." Myrna replied.

"That's what I figured too."

Silence befell them again. They sat, each pretending to read different articles in long forgotten periodicals, occasionally breaking the quiet with small talk. An hour later, Jimmy's two sisters, Ruth and Anna, arrived along with his nephew, Jeffrey. The waiting room became a strange place for a family reunion of sorts.

"You want some coffee, Mama?" Dylan stood stretching his legs and back.

"You going to get something? I'll take a bottle of water if you can find it." Myrna looked at the clock on the wall noting the late hour.

"Okay. Anybody else want anything?"

"I think I'll walk down there with you." Shannon stood and stretched as well. Dylan and she were so much alike in many ways.

"Bring me back a coke." Emma instructed.

"What kind do you want?" Shannon wanted to be clear. They never drank the same kind and she didn't want to hear the complaints if she brought back the wrong one.

"Dr. Pepper."

They left the waiting room in search of vending machines located several floors away. By the time they returned, Dr. Masterson was striding through the doors heading toward the waiting room.

"Glad we came on back. Looks like we got here just in time." Dylan whispered.

"Yeah, it does." Shannon was suddenly nervous but couldn't put her finger on why.

They followed the doctor into the waiting room where their family sat alone and waited.

"Mrs. Watson," Dr. Masterson greeted.

He waited for everyone's attention to settle on him then continued. "We just finished the surgery and your husband is doing fine. He's in recovery now. We got his gallbladder out and it looks like that was what was causing most of the discomfort. It was severely inflamed."

He paused. "But that's not all we found. Since so many of the tests were inconclusive I wanted to make sure there were no other problems. In examining the colon, I found a large mass which appeared to be breaking through the surface. That's why the operation took much longer than expected. We removed the section of colon with the mass and inserted a colostomy bag. It's only a temporary measure. Once the colon heals from the surgery, we can go in a take it out. He should be able to resume normal function after that."

"What about the mass?" Emma wasn't sure about that bit of information.

"That's what we're worried about. I've seen this type of growth before and honestly, it looked bad. I believe the growth may be malignant. I can't say for sure until we get the biopsy back from the lab, but it definitely needed to come out. Once we make sure he's healed up and we can reverse this procedure, we'll be in a better position to determine what treatment needs to follow."

Cancer.

Myrna felt her knees buckle. Dylan and Emma helped her back to her seat as the doctor continued to field questions from the family. Questions that he couldn't answer without more tests.

"I'm afraid I don't know anymore at this time. Once the tests come back, I'll be able to determine what course of action we should take." He turned to Myrna. "I'll be back in the morning to check on him."

She nodded.

He was gone. As quickly as he'd entered and destroyed their lives, he was gone. For a few minutes, no one spoke. Finally, Ruth broke the silence.

"You know, they've come a long way in cancer treatments these days. It's not like when Mama got diagnosed. They only gave her a few months to live. Nowadays people are being treated and cured. He'll probably make a full recovery."

"Yeah, scientists are doing all kinds of research these days." Anna agreed.

Myrna thought back on Jimmy's parents, both of whom passed away from the dreaded 'C' word. Both were in their sixties. Jimmy was only fifty-eight. She also remembered things a little differently than Ruth did. His father had died back in the early '60s, three days after the assassination of John F. Kennedy as a matter of fact. National news made the event impossible to forget especially with so many documentaries on the subject. Every time there was a mention of the famed assassination and conspiracy plots, her mind shot back to them listening to the news on the way to the hospital to see his father for the last time. Jimmy never spoke about it, but she was sure it weighted heavily on his mind as well.

His mother had converted to a Jehovah's Witness some years later and rejected most forms of medicine. She vehemently refused to go to the doctor when the pain started. It wasn't until she had to be carried out in an ambulance that the diagnosis was officially made. By then it was too late. Myrna always wondered if she could have lasted longer, even in those days with the limited treatment options but it was a question she never voiced around Jimmy. The subject of his parent's death was still painful to him. Best not to bring it up. That had been fifteen years ago.

And now her husband had been handed the same fate as his parents. She couldn't think about the possible outcome. It simply couldn't happen that way again. She wasn't ready to lose him yet. He'd be okay. They had caught it in time. Not like his parents. He would be okay. He'd beat it.

"How are you feeling?" Myrna whispered as she gently kissed his forehead.

He looked wane and ashen. His lips were cracked. They hadn't been before. The medicine must have dried them out. "I'm okay."

She lightly stroked his hair as he faded in and out of sleep. The operation had taken over three hours. The nurse said he'd be out of things for most of the night. They were going to move him from recovery to his room once he regained consciousness. She sat with him until the orderlies came to transfer him to the gurney. They wheeled him into his room. Myrna and the kids followed close behind. Once he was settled, Emma went and got a cup of ice from the machine down the hall. Myrna dipped out one piece at a time and placed it in his mouth. It would be a long difficult journey ahead.

CR&O

Dr. Masterson held nothing back in his conversation with Jimmy the next morning. There was no need. Patients often responded better to straightforward information. Once they got over the shock, they were in a better position to move forward with treatment. And if the size of the mass was any indication, Jimmy's treatment would be extensive. Best to go ahead and let him know what he was in for.

CR&O

The grass needed cutting one last time before autumn officially arrived. That's what Jimmy first noticed as he shuffled for his third trip around the house. The doctor had told him that walking was the best way to recover. The quicker he recovered, the quicker he could have the reversal surgery. Walking he could

77

do. Sitting still he could not. The first three days he'd been home, it had rained incessantly the entire time. He had shuffled around the house every thirty minutes or so. Myrna wasn't used to his constant pacing. She wasn't used to his being inside. They were both glad when the rain stopped.

Now that he was out in the fresh air and sunshine, he could at least walk around the house. It was relatively flat and easy to navigate. He had planned on venturing down to the barn and maybe walking around the pasture, but that would take a couple of days to work up to. The doctor had also said to take it easy and Myrna was under the impression that extensive treks to the field to check on the cows violated that directive. It had been the same when he had his back surgery years ago. She wouldn't let him go at his pace. He had to convince her he was ready.

He winched as he sat back down in his recliner and turned on the television. Over five hundred channels from all over the world and the best thing on was old Hee Haw reruns. He turned off the machine, picked up his newest copy of the Farmer's Bulletin, and read about the latest challenges with the bovine industry which reminded him that the calves would be ready to take to market when he was up and about a little better.

"How you feeling, Daddy?" Emma asked as she walked into the den.

"I'm feeling a lot better. Still sore but that's going away." He said looking up from the paper.

"Have you been out walking any?" She inquired.

Myrna shot her a look. "Yes. He's been around the house about twenty times today."

"The doctor said I needed to walk." Jimmy countered.

"He said you needed to take it easy." Myrna tried to put her foot down.

"I am taking it easy. Walking ain't hard."

Emma smiled as Myrna let out a slight huff. "I'm glad you're getting up and around, Daddy."

"I've got an appointment in two weeks for the doctor to look at the incision. I'm hoping he'll go ahead and schedule the next surgery then. I'm ready to get this over with." Jimmy hated being still.

"He said it would probably be a month or so before you could have that." Myrna was worn out trying to doctor such a rambunctious patient.

"Hmph. We'll see. I'm ready to get rid of this thing." There was too much to do to be hindered with such an embarrassing device as a colostomy bag. It had to go. There was no other option.

Jimmy stood up and stretched gingerly. "I think I'll stretch my legs again." And he was gone out the sliding glass door before Myrna could protest.

She shook her head. "That man just cannot sit still. It's about to kill him."

Emma laughed. "It looks like it's about to kill you too."

"I'll be alright if I can ever get him well."

They went into the kitchen to check on the tomato gravy that was cooking. Dylan had come over last night and picked the last of the tomatoes on the vine. He said it didn't look like there'd be anymore. The cucumbers were coming to an end as well. It wouldn't be long before it was time for the turnips and collards to come in. Jimmy was bound and determined to be well before that harvest, even if it killed the both of them.

છ૪ૐ

They were both calm when the doctor told them the tests came back positive. Even still, Myrna couldn't stop the tear that trickled down her cheek. She quickly wiped it away so Jimmy wouldn't see it. He had enough on his plate without worrying about her. He needed all his strength to get well. Dr. Masterson was optimistic. Cancer patients lived much longer these days than they had in the past. New treatments were being found every day. In the past decade, more progress had been made in cancer research and treatment than ever before. The problem was the cancer had progressed to the Stage Four level. They hadn't caught it as early as Myrna had believed. It was actually quite advanced and had breached the exterior wall of the colon. In a way, it was a blessing that Jimmy's gallbladder had inflamed. Without that, they might not have caught it at all. Now they had a fighting chance. Not as good as if it had been found during a routine test, but much better than a few years ago.

Jimmy picked up the referral packet on the way out of the surgeon's office. Dr. Kapel was one of the best oncologists in the region according to Dr. Masterson. They had an appointment for the following week. It had already been made by the receptionist. Jimmy's charts and medical history would be sent over tomorrow. The doctors would discuss treatment options and consult on the best approach to take.

Dr. Kapel's waiting room provided a grim glimpse into Jimmy's future. Patients in varying stages of treatment lined the walls. Some with hair. Most without. All with the gaunt look of a concentration camp prisoner. It was easy to tell the patients from the family members. Family members had the hope of long life.

The treatment program for Jimmy was straightforward. Two types of chemo would be given simultaneously. He would receive twelve treatments, each three weeks apart depending, of course, on how well his body tolerated the drugs. They could adjust the schedule as needed, but the goal was to keep things as close to three weeks apart as possible. He should have the final treatment sometime in the spring.

"When will we begin the treatments?" Jimmy asked.

"We need to get you healed from your next surgery before we officially begin. Dr. Masterson says that you're healing nicely. He should have you scheduled for your reversal operation within a couple of weeks. I want to wait at least a month after that to make sure that everything is working according to plan. Once I get his all clear, we'll set up your first series." Dr. Kapel explained.

As they lay in bed that night, Jimmy turned to Myrna. She was as wide awake as he felt.

"It's going to be okay, you know?"

"I know." She replied. Neither of them believed it.

୧୬ଯ

"Okay, Mr. Watson. We're going to put you under now." The anesthesiologist inserted the clear fluid into the IV.

"Count backwards from ten for me." She instructed leaning close over her patient's face.

Jimmy stared into her hazel eyes. "Ten, nine, eig. . ."

As darkness engulfed his face, he noticed a strange light off to his right. That's odd. He could hear the beeping of the machines around him and the doctor's discussing something rather urgent but he paid little attention. His eyes were focused on the light that continued to grow. It offered warmth and comfort. It was peaceful.

Jimmy turned his head for a better look. He could see a door, one which he had not noticed before when he entered the room. Suddenly, he had the strangest desire to get up and go to the door. He wanted to see where the light on the other side was coming from. Where did the door lead? What did it hold?

He was startled when the door opened and a man walked through. He was unusually dressed in a brown cloak and hood. A monk, perhaps? No. That was ridiculous. There were no monks around here. It's a good thing he didn't try to get up and explore. Must be some kind of costume party over there. That was the last thing he needed during an operation, to try and go to a costume party. They really needed to regulate this hospital better. That had to be a violation of some kind of health code.

The strange man walked over to where Jimmy lay. "Hello, Jimmy." He greeted.

"Hello," Jimmy replied, still unsure why his doctor's had let a party goer into his operation. He watched as the lights in the OR circled the monk's head.

"I've come with a message and to give you a choice." The monk's voice was hypnotic.

"A choice?"

"Yes. Your time in this world is not up. You still have more roads to travel. You can stay until your time or you can leave now. But know this, if you leave now with me, you leave in peace. You will feel no pain. If you choose to stay you will face an agonizing end. Your journey ahead is hard and so the choice is yours. It is yours alone to make."

Suddenly, Jimmy sat up. He could see the doctor's working around him frantically. He stood up and saw himself on the table. It all seemed surreal and yet he understood. He stared at the monk, now silhouetted by the light erupting from the door. The door he hadn't seen before because it hadn't been there. And once he made his decision, it would disappear again, either with him or without.

It was such a peaceful light. Soft and warm. Comforting and embracing. And if what the monk said was true then surely this was the best option. Why face an end of agony and pain?

Then he turned to his left and saw Myrna.

ᝢᝣ

"Mrs. Watson," Dr. Masterson came striding into the waiting room toward the family.

"The operation was a success. We were able to reconstruct the colon. We're going to keep a close eye on him over the next few days to make sure there's no infection but as long as that stays in check everything else looked fine. He should be back to normal in a few weeks."

The girls wrapped their arms around their mother in relief.

"We did have an issue though while he was on the table which is why the procedure took longer than we expected," The doctor continued.

"What kind of an issue?" Myrna wanted all the details.

"Right after he went under, his blood pressure dropped pretty low. It actually got so low that we thought we might lose him at one point. His heart fibrillated. We almost had to shock him, but everything stabilized and we were able to continue with the operation." The doctor was serious but tried to add a soothing air to the conversation. The effort missed its mark.

"What made his heart stop?" Myrna didn't like the sound of any of this.

"It didn't completely stop," Dr. Masterson reassured. "It almost did. It must have been a reaction to the anesthesia. We were able to counteract the reaction and correct the situation."

"Will he have any long term effects from that reaction?" Robby asked. He suspected the answer but was hoping to settle some rattled nerves in the group.

"No. He's fine now. We'll notate his chart so he never receives that anesthesia again, but he should be fine from here on out. He's in recovery now. You should be able to see him in about an hour or so."

The family breathed a collective sigh of relief. All but Myrna who seemed unable to move.

Chapter Five

A CHILLY FOG settled over the pasture. It was cool without being uncomfortable, the perfect weather to walk in. Six weeks had passed since his last surgery. Six weeks since the strange visit from the mysterious cloaked figure. There was no doubt in his mind the experience had been real, but why him? Why now? Why should he be given such a strange choice? He'd never been a particularly religious man. Never one to go to church every Sunday until all this started. Not like Myrna who rarely missed a day. He'd always tried to be a good man but. . .

He paused along the bend in the road where the natural contour of the field curved and followed the tree line. His cows grazed lazily in the distance. He watched them saunter here and there. He loved this land. He loved the freedom it afforded him and the peaceful lifestyle he had built here. Yet, he knew, if the predictions the monk made were true (and he had no reason to doubt they would be) that he would eventually have to part with this land and all these things he loved so much.

His mind drifted to Myrna. He had seen her so clearly that day. Her face had made such a complex decision so easy. How could he miss one minute with her even if that meant some pain in the end? Still he knew his time was short and preparations would have to be made. He had the opportunity to spend more time with Myrna and his children but that also gave him the chance to ensure she was always taken care of. It was an opportunity he wouldn't waste.

CRES

Jimmy read the pamphlet, *How to Prepare for Chemotherapy*, from Dr. Kapel's office once more. It was pretty thorough and addressed things he never would have considered, like going to the dentist. Apparently, chemo leads to increased dental infections. Who in the world would think about that? It talked about the blood work he would need to have the week prior to each treatment and the white blood count levels he would have to maintain. If those levels got too low then the treatments would be postponed until they were adequate. But it went further than just the physical aspects. It talked about childcare and wigs, things Jimmy didn't need to concern himself with, as well as things such as finances and employment. It covered the gamut although not necessarily in the most happy-go-lucky way possible.

Between the two of them, they'd read it at least a dozen times. Myrna wanted to make sure she had everything taken care of. She took the list of foods that helped increase white blood counts to the grocery store and proceeded to buy every pound of beef liver and broccoli within a twenty mile radius. Thankfully, he liked both. He smiled when he thought of the time a few years back when he asked why she didn't make liver as often anymore. He was certain he wouldn't be asking that question any time in the future. She was determined to do everything within her power to keep his iron levels high.

He glanced over at her as she read the latest copy of *Good Housekeeping*. She was worried. He could tell this diagnosis was bothering her although she rarely showed it. Each time she read through the pamphlet, she questioned something they were doing to prepare. She was ready to get this over, get him well, and get on with life.

He looked up from reading as he heard the sliding glass door open up. Dylan and Amy sat down on the loveseat.

"Well, hey. Didn't know y'all were coming over." Myrna put down her magazine.

"We just stopped by to see how you were doing." Dylan replied.

"You ready for tomorrow?" He asked his dad.

"Yeah. They say that shouldn't be too bad. Just putting a port in."

"What all are you going to need me to take care of?" Dylan didn't want to leave anything to chance.

Jimmy thought for a moment. "Just the garden I think. Everything else should be fine."

"You already got enough firewood and everything?" Dylan pressed.

"Should have enough. Still had a good bit from last year."

"I'll get you some extra cut." Dylan preferred more hands on projects than his

90

brother who excelled in the office end of business affairs.

"Come on down to the barn with me. I've got to feed the cows anyway. I'll show you what I've already got. It should be enough." Jimmy stood up and reached for his ball cap before the two men headed to the barn.

"How's Mama doing?" Dylan asked when they were well out of earshot.

"She's doing good. She's worried, but you know she never really says anything." Jimmy was honest.

"Well, chemo is kind of a serious thing. Most people would be worried about it."

"Yeah."

He looked over at his father who seemed oddly at peace. "You aren't worried?"

Jimmy shook his head. "No. Not really."

"Why?"

Jimmy didn't immediately answer. He stared off into the distance lost in deep thought. Finally he turned to Dylan, "You probably ain't going to believe this," he opened before recounting the entire story of his unusual visit. He watched for any signs that his son might mock him or harbor any doubt. But Dylan simply nodded. His dad was not one for fancy. If he said he got visited, then he got visited.

"So you're going to be okay for awhile?" Dylan finally replied.

"I suspect so." Jimmy agreed.

"Well, I'm still going to cut you some more wood." Dylan looked at the half cord stacked and covered underneath the shelter. That would never be enough for a really good cold snap and the weather forecasters were predicting a rough winter. Dad wouldn't be able to get enough wood put away before then and he surely didn't need to catch anything while he was going through his treatments. It was simple. Monk or no monk, they needed some more firewood. Best to go ahead and be prepared for the worst.

ᏣᎦᏉ

The wet autumn leaves underfoot made no sound as the trio traipsed across the vacant lot. Bill didn't mind getting out of the office. It was the part of his job that he enjoyed most. And this piece of property wasn't as bad as he'd told Jimmy in the beginning. Actually, it reminded him of his family's old homestead a few miles away. All the property in this area had the same rustic feel. Jimmy and Robby had done a good job with the property division. Each lot was over an acre and had the added benefit of mature hardwoods. Very few properties in the area had that combination. They were much desired. He'd shown these pieces dozens of times and the Lord only knew how many people came out here to look without him.

But no matter how diligently he worked to finalize the deal, nobody seemed willing to buy. He'd recently started taking an informal survey of the potential buyers to try to weed out any negative selling points. There was only one. Nobody wanted to pay full price. Some didn't have that much to invest or couldn't get the financing needed. Others realized how much of an investment it would be to buy property and then try to build something yourself. Others thought the price was too dear. They'd seen the latest program on cable which promised to show viewers how ordinary people could flip all kinds of property for huge returns. Several people actually mentioned the show as inspiration. If the economy itself wasn't bad enough, the entire television community was out to sabotage the sell and transfer of this property.

CRBO

The first two rounds of chemotherapy went much better than anyone expected. Myrna's iron rich diet plan helped him keep his white blood cells at a higher than expected level. Dr. Kapel had prescribed anti-nausea medication just in case but so far the bottle sat on his nightstand unopened. He was determined to keep it that way as long as possible.

"Something sure smells good." He greeted as he walked into the kitchen.

"It's the turkey. I put it in the oven a couple of hours ago. Shouldn't take too much longer before it'll be ready." Myrna was mixing the cornbread and didn't look up.

"I know it'll be good." Jimmy left as quickly as he arrived. In the den, he sat in his recliner for a moment. The smell of turkey roasting never made him queasy before but then he'd never had a chemo treatment two days before Thanksgiving either. Maybe he should have followed Myrna's advice and insisted that the treatment be after the holiday when there wouldn't be so many smells floating through the house.

By the time the cornbread was browning in the oven, the effects of Jimmy's third treatment hit with full force. He spent much of the remainder of the afternoon lying in bed, hoping to avoid as many of the odors that permeated the house as possible. Keeping the bedroom door closed worked well enough for awhile but even that tactic couldn't withstand the full force of the onslaught.

"Do you want me to call everyone and tell them not to come over tomorrow?" Myrna asked as she stroked his hair.

"No. I'll be alright." He held a heating pad close by to ease some of the knots his stomach was tied in.

"Are you sure? I don't mind calling everybody." Myrna was empathic.

"I'll be okay. This can't last forever." He winched slightly.

She wasn't so sure. "Have you taken any of your medicine?"

"Yeah. I took some about an hour ago. It helped a good bit."

He still didn't look good but at least he was able to rest for a few minutes now. She let him sleep for over an hour before Robby called to check in.

"You know, we don't have to come over there tomorrow. I can call everybody and tell them to make other arrangements."

"No, Jimmy wants y'all to come to the house. He said he'll be fine."

"Saying you're going to be fine and being fine are two different things." Robby reminded her.

"I know, but you know your dad."

Thanksgiving celebrations were much more subdued that year. Jimmy stayed in his room, only making an appearance once dinner was completely on the table. He'd taken the maximum dosage of medication that morning to help stave off any lingering effects but the medicine would only do so much. He nibbled here and there, forcing himself to eat far more than he wanted. After dinner, he visited with his kids for a few minutes before venturing back to his room. Emma and Shannon cleaned up the kitchen while Robby and Dylan went down to the barn to tend to the cows, each party waiting until they were out of earshot from either parent before drafting plans for helping their parents manage the chores around the farm.

 CRBO

"Hey, old man. I think I got you an early Christmas present."

Jimmy could use some good news. These last two treatments had taken their toll. He couldn't remember feeling more washed out. "You do? What is it?"

"I just got an offer faxed over for one of your vacant lots." Bill announced proudly.

"That's real good news." Jimmy felt a sense of relief he wasn't expecting.

"I thought that might cheer you up a little." Bill smiled.

"That cheers me up a lot."

"So how are you feeling?"

"Honestly, I've been better." For those who knew Jimmy well, it was a monumental admission.

"It's getting pretty rough on you, isn't it?"

"Yeah, it is."

"Is there anything you or Myrna need me to do? You know I'll do anything for you." Bill repeated the offer he made every time they talked.

"You can sell the rest of those lots." Jimmy smiled.

"I'm working on that one as hard as I can."

"I know."

"You want me to run this offer out to you to look at? I hate for you to have to get out in this weather."

"No. I'll run up there. I need to get out of the house for a little bit. I'm driving Myrna crazy." He was driving himself crazy from being inside so much.

C33O

Myrna and Jimmy sat down at the modest conference table and listened as Neil Portman outlined a comprehensive estate plan for them both. It was far more complex than Myrna imagined. She thought they were only updating their wills, and a will was certainly part of it. Neil was under the impression that they needed trusts and healthcare directives. It was a bit overwhelming.

He gave them some forms and questionnaires to answer before their next meeting. She flipped through the papers as Neil answered some of Jimmy's questions. The questions were highly personal. Far more personal than she liked to get with anyone. She knew he was their attorney and was representing them but still, some things you liked to keep to yourself. Thankfully, Jimmy could handle all of that. He enjoyed that sort of thing.

Besides, once everything was completed, Jimmy wouldn't worry so much about her future. It would give him tremendous peace of mind. She could tell it was a question that had bothered him since this ordeal began. He'd already read two books from the library on the topic. Now he was ready to finalize the paperwork. Once all this was completed, he could focus on more important things like getting well. And that was what was actually important.

CB80

Nora Braxton was sitting at her desk calculating the monthly payroll expenses when the bell on the front door chimed. She wasn't expecting anyone today and had received no calls requesting their services. It was supposed to be the perfect quiet morning to catch up on the mounds of paperwork that littered her desk. Oh well. Maybe this wouldn't take too long.

She emerged from her office to find him standing there. A simple farmer by the looks of him; tall, graying dark brown hair, beige work pants, and a red flannel shirt. His clothing was a bit heavy for such a warm spring day. He completed the ensemble with a blue baseball cap advertising the feed he used for his cows. His wire frame glasses perched securely on a proud English nose.

"Good morning. I'm Nora Braxton," she extended her hand. "How can I help you?"

Jimmy returned the greeting cordially. "I'm Jimmy Watson. I was wondering if I could talk to you for a few minutes."

"Of course," she smiled pleasantly. "May I ask what about?"

"I need to make some funeral arrangements."

"I'm sorry to hear that. For a loved one?"

"No. For me." He stated plainly.

She often advised people to begin end of life planning in advance but few people ever heeded that advice. Especially farmers. They tended to think about the day-to-day tasks of running a farm, the price of seeds, and the possible profitability of their crops. End of life decisions never occurred until, well, the end of life. Now she feared the man standing opposite her may be faced with that prospect and undergoing some difficult challenges.

"Why don't we step into my office?" She motioned him through the door and moved to hastily clear the paperwork from her desk, excusing the mess and making small talk as she did so.

"You said you'd like to start making your funeral arrangements, Mr. Watson?" She asked as she took the appropriate forms from the side desk drawer.

"May I ask what got you thinking about end of life preparations?"

Jimmy took a deep breath and hesitated slightly before answering her question. "I had a recent cancer scare and I'm going to be taking my last round of chemotherapy next week. The doctors say it could comeback in a few years and I want to make sure everything is taken care of when the time comes."

"I'm sorry to hear you've been sick." Nora always hated the bad news that accompanied her job.

Jimmy quietly nodded his appreciation for her concern. Together they went over all the options and payment plans. By the end of the meeting, Jimmy had set up a payment plan for both Myrna and himself. He knew she had more time on this old world than he did but even so, that would be one less thing to worry about when the time came. Services would be completely paid for in three years time. He wrote a check for the down payment and thanked Nora for her time.

CRBO

Jimmy read an article in the Farmer's Bulletin as the chemicals dripped through the IV and into his veins. New methods were being developed to increase production in draught stricken areas. It would be very beneficial here since the state had been in a water shortage for the last two years. He'd only put a few things in the ground so far this season. There was still time to implement some of the suggestions in the article. He dog-eared it for later reference.

"You doing okay, Mr. Watson?" The nurse asked as she checked the IV.

"So far. But I'll be doing a lot better once this last round is over." He smiled.

"I know you will. You've done really good with your treatments. A lot better than some of the patients we see. We're going to miss you around here."

Jimmy fidgeted in his chair a little. "Y'all are nice and all but I'm not going to miss this place. I can't wait to see it in my rear view mirror for the last time."

"I don't blame you one bit. If I didn't work here, I sure wouldn't want to walk through those doors." She stated without the slightest trepidation.

೮ஜ೮

They waited for over an hour for their name to be called. It was the final scheduled appointment with Dr. Kapel. The last time they hoped they would see him for many, many years. Jimmy had taken all the tests last week. Now, they hoped to hear the news they longed for.

"Good morning, Jimmy," Dr. Kapel shook his hand. "Mrs. Watson," He took hers in turn.

"Good morning." They each replied.

"I have the results from your tests and I'm sorry, or that is I'm happy to say I won't be

102

seeing you for quite some time. You are completely healthy." He beamed.

Myrna let out a relieved breath and fought back tears of joy.

"That's great to hear!" Jimmy broke out into a large smile. This nightmare was over. Now he could start working on his to-do list which had grown exponentially over the last few months.

"Yes, it is!" Myrna draped her arm around Jimmy's shoulder.

"We'll still need you to come back every six months for evaluation. We want to keep an eye on your blood work to make sure nothing comes back, but as of right now, it looks like the treatments worked beautifully and you are free to continue life as before." The doctor couldn't stop the smile on his face.

"Yeah, I don't want this again anytime soon." Jimmy agreed.

"Have you followed up with Dr. Masterson's office?" Dr. Kapel scribbled some notes in the chart.

"We had an appointment with him last month. He said everything looked good from the X-rays. Nothing to worry about." Myrna confirmed.

"Good. You'll also need to follow up with his office. I recommend six month intervals for him as well. If anything does come back, we want to make sure we catch it earlier this time." He peered over his glasses at the pair of them. "But as of right now you're good."

They floated on joy out of the office. It was a bittersweet feeling passing all those other people who were sitting in there waiting on less than pleasant news. Even still, neither could remember being that happy in years.

Myrna let out another sigh of relief as she sat down in the passenger's seat and buckled the belt. "This is the best day we've had in a long time." She smiled at Jimmy.

"Feels pretty good, doesn't it?" He flashed a wide grin.

"You know, I feel like celebrating." She announced.

"You do?" Jimmy stared at her. They didn't often vary from their routine.

"Yeah."

"Where do you want to go?"

She thought for awhile. "Let's go to Cracker Barrel. We haven't been there in forever."

"That sounds good." Jimmy pulled out of the parking lot and headed down the road.

Chapter Six

"NO! YOU CAN'T drive over my car like that!" James growled.

"Yeah I can. We're going to make them explode." Wayne rammed the cars together once more, aggravating his brother to no end. The twins were in the middle of an epic mix of racing and destruction.

Jimmy sat reading his newspaper while Emma and Myrna chatted about some recipes they'd discovered. Directly, Jimmy flicked the paper allowing the corner edge to fold down slightly. He peered around the edge at the children. They were becoming too rambunctious. Emma knew the signal well.

"Boys, either settle down or go outside." She told them sternly.

"But it's hot outside." Wayne protested. He enjoyed tormenting James at every opportunity.

"Then settle down." She was unrelenting.

"Okay." They agreed but with a great sense of martyrdom. She'd stopped them just when things were about to get good.

Jimmy flicked the corner of his paper once more, returning it to its original position and continued reading. Emma and Myrna continued the conversation as if nothing had transpired. When he was finished reading, he folded it neatly and sat it between the two chairs. Myrna would want to read it later. He picked up his ball cap and headed for the door.

"Come on and go with me to feed the cows." He motioned for the boys who were now sullenly playing with their cars.

"Can we ride on the trailer?" James was up first.

"Yeah."

That caught Wayne's interest. "Me too."

"Both of you can if y'all come on." And they were gone, off to help with all the adventures of farm life with their grandfather.

"Dad seems to be doing a lot better." Emma said as she watched them stepping off the porch.

"Yeah, he's getting back to his old self now. Those treatments were rough on him though."Myrna admitted.

"I'm just glad it's behind him now."

"What are those boxes over there, Grandpa?" Wayne asked as they walked down to the barn.

"Those are my bee hives."

"I don't like bees," James said.

"Why not?" Jimmy always seemed to be on the less popular side of these striped insects.

"I got stung by one last summer." James explained.

"That's no reason to hate all bees. Bees are important. We wouldn't be able to eat without them." Jimmy countered.

"No they're not. They're just bugs." Wayne wanted to provide the voice of experience and reason.

"They are important." Jimmy began to tell the boys about the role bees played in farming and how honey was produced. He walked them down to the garden where some of the peas and cucumbers were starting to bloom to show them the different parts of the flower and how pollen is transported from one section to the other. That was the great thing about grandpa. He could make anything interesting.

On the way back from their adventure, he offered to let the boys see the bees up close if they were really good. He had been meaning to check on his hives anyway. They didn't seem to be producing like he thought they should. He wanted to find out what was wrong with them so he'd have enough honey for the winter. The boys couldn't resist the chance to operate the smoker while Jimmy showed them the inner workings of a real live bee's nest. None of the kids at school had done that.

⁂

"Are Emus the New Answer to the Beef Shortage?" It was an intriguing question that Jimmy had never pondered. The article in the Farmer's Bulletin made a convincing argument. The bird was a staple of meat in Australia and New Zealand. As popular as beef the writer said. They ate less, took less time to mature, and required less of a land investment. There was no extensive grazing area required. Five acres of land filled with emus could produce the meat equivalent of twenty acres worth of beef cattle. Farmers and ranchers across the country were investing in these imported birds. As beef prices continued to rise, emu meat would become a major player in grocery stores across the country.

It was an interesting notion. He reread the article twice through. He didn't know much about emus other than they looked a lot like ostriches. He studied the picture accompanying the article. They were ugly, that's for sure. But most creatures couldn't help how ugly they were. He wouldn't hold that against them. After all, some of the best dogs he ever had were ugly as sin.

"I'm going for my walk," Myrna mentioned as she slipped on her walking shoes and headed for the door.

"Have a good time." Jimmy replied.

He returned to his article about immigrant birds and wondered if they really were the America's hope for the forecasted beef shortage. It wasn't unheard of to bring in foreign crops to supplement regional food chains. Different breeds of cattle were often crossbred with local stock to improve the herd. It made sense that emus could be imported to offset a potential shortage.

The county extension office didn't keep a lot of information on file about emus. As a matter of fact, they didn't keep any. Apparently, Jimmy was the only person to ever ask about the flightless birds.

"I can do some research and try to find you some information on them if you like." The extension agent offered.

"Do that for me, please." Jimmy replied.

"Sure thing. Is there anything else I can help you with today?"

"What do you know about bees?" Jimmy asked. His hives weren't producing honey as expected. He had done all he knew to do. Now it was time to call in the experts.

"You having problems with your hive?"

"Yeah."

The agent was in familiar territory now. "The first thing you have to do is to make sure you have a queen. They won't produce without a queen."

Jimmy nodded. "I got a queen."

"They do better if they're facing toward the south."

"That's the way I've got them turned." Jimmy nodded again.

"Do you have enough pollen sources for them?" The agent went through his mental checklist.

"I think I do. My wife has about four nice sized flower beds around there. I have my garden which is about a half acre in size. We've got a bunch of fruit trees and that big ol' flowering cherry tree at the side of the house." Jimmy tried to recollect if there were any more

110

major sources in the area but couldn't remember any.

"That should be enough." The agent agreed. He thought a little harder.

"We do recommend having more than one hive." He grasped at the last straw available.

"I have eight hives." Jimmy replied. "How many do I need?"

The agent was somewhat ashen. "And each one has a queen?"

"Yeah."

"Maybe I should research some additional information on bees as well."

"I'd appreciate that."

CRO

Shannon sat down in the rocker opposite her father and observed him as he carefully stuffed an empty matchbox with tissues. He then placed his watch in the box before tearing a sheet of paper from his legal pad, folding it neatly, and putting it in the box as well.

"What are you doing, Daddy?" Curiosity finally got the better of her.

"I'm going to send my watch back." He responded looking over his wire framed glasses.

She studied him carefully. The watch was at least as old as she was. She couldn't remember him without it.

"Back where?"

"To the factory."

"Why?"

"It stopped working."

"Well, it's old. Maybe it's time for you to buy a new one." She suggested.

"Why?" Now he was perplexed. "It has a lifetime warranty on it. They're supposed to fix it if it ever stops working. And it stopped working."

Shannon looked over at her mom who only shrugged. How do you argue with that kind of logic?

☽☾

Jimmy studied the papers Bill presented for the closing. They all seemed to be in order although he double-checked the numbers with his pocket calculator before signing the forms. Bill was a good man but he was human. Anyone could make a mistake. He'd learned long ago to check the figures before agreeing to anything.

The third lot had finally sold. Only seven more to go. The widow lady buying this lot said she fell in love with the place the moment she stepped foot on it. She couldn't wait to build a home here. She loved the trees and all the quiet it provided. And it was cheaper than any of the lots she'd looked at before. It was the perfect fit.

Bill smiled over at Jimmy while she spoke. He couldn't understand it. These parcels should be flying off the market but he couldn't get them to move the way they should. The price was reasonable, more than reasonable from what they just heard. He jotted down a reminder to make a few phone calls after the closing. Maybe some of his friends in the business could help get the word out.

⟨⟩⟨⟩

> *Dear Sir,*
> *Enclosed please find the watch that I have had for quite some time. It stopped working last week. As per your company's lifetime guarantee, I would like to have it fixed.*
> > *Sincerely,*
> > *Jimmy Watson*

Elias set the letter aside and pulled the antique wristwatch from the box. He'd worked for Timex for almost twenty years and had only seen this model twice before. A quick search of his reference manuals told him they stopped manufacturing it in 1959. Assuming he'd bought it new, Mr. Watson had indeed owned it for some time.

He studied the timepiece in great detail. The face was well worn. Scratches and abrasions covered the glass surface. One long crack stretched from ten to six. The Roman 'V' had broken free and now aimlessly wandered about with each movement. Apparently these minor cosmetic issues hadn't warranted a return to the factory. He turned it over to study its belly. The screws attaching the back cover were rusted beyond the point of recognition. Sweat stains dyed the olive nylon band creating a myriad of strange patterns. The band was frayed along the edges in several places. This was the watch of a laborer, by the looks of it. Someone who knew the importance of work and the value of a dollar. Elias felt an instant appreciation for Jimmy Watson. Men like him were a rarity these days. Like this watch, Jimmy was an antique. And antiques must be cherished.

ೞ

Jimmy stopped by Braxton's on his way to Atlanta to pick up his new investment. With the final payment made to Braxton's (well over a year ahead of schedule), that item was off his shoulders and he could focus on other things.

114

The church counsel had begun looking at the possibility of building a new sanctuary and turning the current building into a fellowship hall. It was a good idea and high time for such an investment. He had promised to draw up some ideas for them to look at. It would be a big project for their little church although it was nothing he hadn't handled before.

As soon as he picked up his emus and got them settled in, he would start working something up for them to see. With any luck, he should have everything sketched out by Sunday. He would at least have enough drawn to give them an idea of what the new building would look like.

⚬⚭⚬

Heath couldn't wait to show off his new learner's permit. After begging his dad to go on his first official driving lesson, they decided to head over to his grandparents house to complete the celebration. Jake decided to come along to provide some harmless brotherly teasing from the backseat of the Tahoe.

"Good, I'm glad y'all are here." Jimmy smiled, meeting them at the door.

"It's official, Grandpa," Heath beamed. "I'm a driver."

Jimmy looked at the laminated card in the boy's hand. It didn't seem like he should be old enough to be in high school let alone drive.

"That's real good, Heath. I'm proud of you, son." Jimmy nodded his approval.

"Where's Grandma? I want to show her."

Jimmy jerked his head toward the den. "She's in there shelling peas."

Heath ran off to brag some more, leaving his father and brother to talk to his granddad.

"Looks like you were about to go somewhere." Robby commented.

"Yeah. I was just about to walk out the door. Jake, go get Heath and y'all can go with me."

"Where you going?" Robby asked.

"Gotta go get some hay. Mr. Hartfield called this morning and he's baling it today. I want to get it in the barn before it rains tomorrow."

"Okay."

"You think Heath will want to drive?" Jimmy grinned sideways at his oldest.

Robby chuckled. "Oh yeah."

When the boys returned, Jimmy handed Heath the keys to his old Ford. "Y'all come on."

"You want us to follow you over there?" Robby asked already opening the driver's side door of his SUV.

"Unless you want to ride on top." His dad commented over his shoulder as he climbed into the passenger side.

Heath started the pickup truck but paused before putting it in gear at his grandfather's dire warning.

"Don't hit your grandmother's car." Jimmy said sternly to the youth.

Heath looked over the elder's shoulder at the white Cadillac parked in the other slot in the carport. He didn't really want to know what would happen if he damaged it. He suspected it wouldn't be good.

"Yes, sir." He mumbled and slowly reversed the vehicle out.

They drove a few miles away to the Hartfield farm. Jimmy got out at the gate, leaving Heath inside. He talked briefly with Ben Hartfield before motioning Heath through.

"Drive along that first row of bales. We're going to load them up while you drive. Once we load the bales, you pull up to the next one. Got it?"

"Yes, sir." Heath smiled to himself. This was alright. He got to drive while everyone else was out in the heat loading hay. A driver's license had its advantages.

Unfortunately, it didn't have a working radio. Heath turned the knob to every conceivable spot on the dial to no avail. Then

117

he realized the antenna was missing. There was no telling where or when it had disappeared. He was also not allowed to use the air conditioning. Jimmy saw no need to run the AC while Heath was sitting in there with the windows rolled down. That was just a waste of gas even if the temperature did top ninety degrees. They could turn it back on when they drove home, but there was no need to use it before.

Jimmy stood in the bed while Robby and Jake threw bales over the side. He had to arrange each one in a specific manner to maximize the load capacity. As soon as the bed was filled to the edges, Jimmy stacked a row that jutted out about six inches from the side. Another row followed adding six more inches to the side. The cab completely disappeared after the next row. Several more rows followed in similar fashion before he rounded the formation.

"Ain't that enough, Grandpa?" Jake yelled up at Jimmy.

Robby laughed heartily. "Nope. He can get another fifty bales up there."

Actually, Jimmy managed to fit sixty-two more bales on the truck. He secured the whole thing with a few straps of twine. It was packed in tight. It wasn't going anywhere.

"Don't hit any bumps too fast." Jimmy warned Heath. The blue two toned Ford now sat considerably closer to the ground.

Robby wiped the sweat from his brow. They followed the giant hay mushroom back to the barn. Heath was gingerly backing in when they arrived. All his mirrors were blocked; he only had Jimmy's instructions to guide him.

"Climb on up to the top and throw them down when I tell you." Jimmy instructed Jake. Robby's oldest son did as instructed. Once atop the mound, he sat on the rafters awaiting further instruction. His feet never leaving the stack below.

Jimmy was just as particular stacking his hay in the barn as he had been loading his truck. Robby knew his system well. Heath picked it up quickly enough to avoid getting in the way. With the four of them working together, the hay was unloaded and stored to Jimmy's strict specifications within thirty minutes. When they finished, Jimmy walked over to the water hose and drank a liberal amount of water.

"Okay, y'all get something to drink if you want it, and then let's go get the second load."

 భ

The church council met two weeks later to discuss the sketches Jimmy had submitted. They loved the details he incorporated into the rough draft. Only a few minor changes were suggested here and there. Jimmy had an eye for building. He had already addressed numerous issues the committee never would have thought of on their own. After years of owning a successful contracting firm, he was well versed in all the state and local codes which would need to be considered.

Unfortunately, they didn't like the costs projections he submitted along with the drawings. It was considerably more expensive than they had hoped it would be. It was more than double what they thought they could realistically raise and pay for the new addition.

"We're in the middle of a building boom. The prices for materials keep going up every year. If you want to build a new sanctuary, it will never be cheaper than it is now." Jimmy offered his opinion to the board.

"But how will we pay for it?" Abigail Freeman wanted to know.

"We could always get a loan." Jeff Anderson suggested.

"No. That's the last thing we need to do." Horace Smith was firm.

"Either way you go, you're going to have to get a loan for the construction." Jimmy jumped in. "You can't start a project like this without one. It really just depends on whether you decide to borrow what you need or try to squeak by with the bare minimum."

The members contemplated his words for a moment.

"But, I'm telling you now, if you just try to squeak by, you will not get the end results you want. You might as well not even try to do it."

"What if we decided to wait another year? Abigail liked to explore all the options. "How much more would it cost then?"

"There's no way of knowing what prices will do. They could plummet in that time but I doubt it. If they continue the way they've gone for the last three to five years, this building will probably cost ten percent more to build based solely on how the market has gone." Jimmy had worked the numbers several times over. They'd be lucky if it only cost an extra ten percent.

It was not the information any of the members wanted to hear. They discussed the options for another hour before tabling the decision until the next meeting. Some serious contemplation would need to be done before agreeing to such a monumental project.

⊙₰⊙

The postman delivered the watch two weeks later. Myrna almost didn't recognize it. The glass had been completely buffed and polished. The Roman numerals replaced. The face was cleaned and shone in the afternoon sun. Only the band reminded her of the battered old relic that Jimmy had mailed off weeks ago. The old sweat stained strap had been replaced by a brand new olive green nylon band. It was definitely Jimmy's watch.

Jimmy took the note from the case.

> *This should do you for the next thirty years.*
>
> *Regards,*
> *Elias*

He handed the note to his wife and stared at his newly repaired watch. "Looks like he did a good job."

"Yeah. He did." That was a bit of an understatement in Myrna's opinion.

Chapter Seven

EMUS PROVED TO be somewhat more troublesome than Jimmy was first led to believe. For one thing, they made a God awful racket that drove a man to distraction. It was a strange knocking sort of noise that started in the toes of their feet and rumbled its way up to their necks where it stayed and echoed around for about twenty minutes.

If that wasn't bad enough, they just happened to be the dumbest animals ever to set foot on Earth. He couldn't put them out in the field because they were too stupid to come and eat at feeding time. He had to fix up the pins and keep them shut up so he could make sure they ate on a regular basis.

He couldn't fault the poor things for being ugly. After all, some creatures were just born homely. But the sheer idiocy of these birds was beyond reason. No creature should be dumber than a turkey. He was just thankful it hadn't come down a good downpour since he got them. He was certain they were going to drown if he couldn't figure out how to rig an umbrella to their necks.

∞

Myrna patted her hands on the dish towel as she reached for the phone.

"Jimmy, it's Marion from down the road." She handed him the receiver.

"Hello."

"Good morning, Jimmy. How are you doing today?" Marion greeted.

"Good. How are you?"

"Well, I'm a little confused."

"What's got you confused?" Jimmy sat back and watched Myrna sip her coffee.

"Because I woke up this morning and found three of the ugliest birds I've ever laid eyes on out in the middle of my field. And I was wondering if you'd finally decided to get rid of those overgrown turkeys."

"No I hadn't planned on getting rid of them just yet. I kinda figured on keeping them a little while longer."

"Well, can you take them back? They've got my chickens in a terrible uproar with all that racket they keep making." Marion Morrison owned the largest chicken farm in the county. His pasture was nestled in the dell below four industrial sized chicken houses. Jimmy could only imagine the ruckus that was going on if those emus were producing an echo up in those houses. Add that to the clatter that normally went on with the yard birds and it was sure to be an earsplitting experience.

"Yeah, let me get one of my sons out here and we'll be down there in just a bit." He laid the phone down and looked back over at Myrna.

"The emus got out?" She asked before he answered her questioning look.

"Yeah."

"How'd they get all the way down to Marion's?"

He shook his head. "I guess they got out and just kept wandering 'til they got to a field with cows in it." Jimmy's matter-of-fact manner thinly veiling his growing contempt for those birds. He took another sip of his coffee.

"Well, let me call Robby and see if he can send one of his men down here to help."

Robby didn't bat an eye at the conversation with his dad. It hadn't been a call he was anticipating but knowing his dad's ability to find interesting projects, it wasn't totally unexpected either.

"I've got a meeting with the city this afternoon that I can't miss but I'll send someone down there." They spoke for a few moments more before he hung up the phone and thought about his ongoing construction projects.

"Hey C.J., come here for a minute." He called to the office across the hall.

"Yeah, what do you need?" C.J. leaned against the door frame.

"What do you have going on today?"

"Nothing pressing today. We finished up that renovation yesterday. I was going to have my guys clean up the stockyard. It's gotten a bit unmanageable lately."

"Yeah. It has." Robby thought for a moment.

"I tell you what, get your guys started on that and then you head down to Daddy's house. He has something he needs some help with."

126

"I know how your dad is. Do I need to take somebody with me?"

Robby nodded sagely. "You might want to do that." There was no need for too many details. C.J. would figure it out when he got there. Why spoil all the fun?

Marcus accompanied C.J. down to Mr. Watson's farm for the project. C.J. liked Marcus and had begun taking some extra time with him, teaching him more of the ropes of the construction business with each passing day. Unlike some of his peers, he was a quick learner and a hard working young man. Late twenties, tall and broad shouldered, he was an excellent addition to have on any jobsite. They pulled into the drive and headed toward Mr. Watson's barn. C.J. rolled down the window when he saw Mr. Watson walking down the hill.

"Good morning, Mr. Watson. How are you doing?"

"Good. How are you, C.J.?"

"Good. This is Marcus. Robby said we might need some help for this project. What are we going to do?" He looked ahead and saw the cattle trailer attached to Mr. Watson's old Ford.

"My birds got loose and went down to Morrison's chicken farm. We've got to go get 'em."

Marcus stared at Mr. Watson for a second before turning his attention to C.J. who was looking equally perplexed.

"You must have a lot of birds to catch if you need a trailer that big." C.J. once again stared at the cattle trailer.

"No. Only three." Jimmy stated dryly. Before there could be any further delays, he turned and headed for his truck.

As they drove down the road toward the Morrison farm, Marcus became increasingly concerned. "Did he say that we only needed to catch three birds?"

C.J. nodded. "That's what he said."

"How big are those birds?"

"I don't exactly know, but they must be substantial." C.J. bit the inside of his lip, a nervous habit he'd developed since he quit smoking.

They pulled into Marion's place and following the dirt road along the edge of the field until they came to the gate. Jimmy got out and motioned for Marcus to join him. He could see Marion making his way down from the top chicken house. A friendly wave indicated Marion would be down as soon as he finished up the work with his hens.

"Once we drive through, close the gate back and then we'll get started." He instructed Marcus.

"Yes, sir." Marcus was growing more concerned by the moment.

Jimmy pulled far enough into the pasture to allow both trucks in while maintaining easy access to the trailer. Catching an emu could be challenging but he was hoping that it wouldn't take all day. He had several other things he wanted to get to and this little distraction was interfering with his schedule. When C.J. came around to his truck, Jimmy was already pulling out several old pillowcases and lengths of rope from the backseat.

"Here you go. You'll probably need this." He handed a pillowcase and rope to C.J. and then to Marcus when he walked up.

"Why?" C.J. studied the items then fixed his gaze on Mr. Watson.

"So we can catch my birds."

"Mr. Watson, if we're going to put them in this then why did you need that big ol' trailer?" C.J. finally voiced his growing concern for Mr. Watson's sanity.

Marcus waited on baited breath for the answer.

Jimmy looked C.J. square in the face and without the slightest hint of sarcasm said, "That ain't to put the birds in. That's to go over

129

their heads. And then we'll use the rope as a leash and lead them back to the trailer."

"To go over their heads?"

"Yeah. They should be easier to lead that way." Jimmy shut the driver's side door of his truck and scanned the field looking for his wayward flock.

"What kinda birds are we catching?" Fear began to grow in C.J.'s voice.

"Emus."

"A What?"

"What's a emu?" Marcus could no longer restrain his unease.

"That thing over there." Jimmy pointed to his right where some fifty yards away stood his lost fowl.

C.J. and Marcus both stared unbelievingly at the bird. Slowly Marcus began to inch back as if hoping to disappear somewhere into the background. The current task at hand caused him a fair amount of trepidation.

"Mr. Watson, I . . . I don't know nuthin about catchin' no six foot turkey!" He was reaching for the door handle of the truck.

"That's okay. There's no better time to learn." Jimmy replied. "Come on. Let's go. I got some stuff around the house I gotta do this afternoon."

C.J. looked over at Marcus who was trying desperately to blend into the paint on the truck. "Come on. It'll be alright, Marcus."

"I don't know about that."

C.J. smiled. "Didn't you used to play football?"

"Not against no ostrich, I didn't!"

They followed Jimmy as he eased up on the emu, one considerably more reluctant than the other.

"Now we need to take them one at a time and kinda surround them. We want to try to box them in 'cause the last thing I want to do is to get in a foot race with these things." Jimmy instructed when the other two caught up.

"We'll ease up on him and two of us will grab him while the other one throws the pillowcase over its head.

Marcus and C.J. couldn't think of a better plan on the spur of the moment so they agreed. Marcus flanked to the right, C.J. to the left. Jimmy stayed put and made every effort to stare the critter down. The two flanks were closing in when the bird got spooked and bolted. Undeterred, Jimmy had them try again. And again. And again. Finally on the fifth try, one bird was being led back to the trailer by the end of a rope wearing a particularly lovely floral print pillowcase.

The next two birds proved considerably more difficult to capture. Despite being dumber than two rocks thrown together, they were both reluctant to don Jimmy's choice of head wear. Each time the men came within ten feet of either animal, they scampered off.

Marion and his son, Chris, came down to join the chase. The younger Morrison had been active in the local FFA during high school and fancied himself a rodeo star. He decided to bring his talents with a lasso, limited as they may be, to the adventure. After the third attempt, he made his goal and a melee of epic proportions ensued. As the rope cinched around the scrawny neck of the fowl, the bird decided to charge Marcus who began to wave his floral pillowcase with abandon. That succeeded in stopping the initial pursuit long enough for C.J. to lunge at the back of the bird. Like a bullet, the emu shot off dragging Chris along behind and C.J. riding on its back.

"Hold on to him!" Marion and Jimmy hollered in unison. They, along with Marcus, gave chase and wrestled the bird into submission about twenty yards away.

As they secured the second bird in the trailer, Jimmy looked over at C.J. "Did you enjoy your ride?"

C.J. shook his head. "I'm hoping it's the only time I'm gonna have to ride one of those damn birds today." Some of the fun was wearing off of this little escapade.

"Chris, next time try to rope him around his feet." Marion instructed his son as they took a short breather.

"Yes, sir."

"You think he'll be able to get the rope around the bird's feet?" Jimmy wasn't fully convinced of Chris' roping ability.

"If he can't we can set a trap for him. Lay the noose down and pull it when he steps inside." C.J. was looking for any viable alternative to taking another ride.

"That might work better." Marion agreed.

"What do you think, Marcus?" C.J. had noticed his apprentice was not exactly proactive in the emu roundup.

Marcus still hovered around the background. "Just as long as I don't have to ride that thing." He made a mental note to start looking at some college courses to expand his employment opportunities.

The final emu must have heard the game plan. He watched with a sense of amused curiosity as Chris laid the noose on the ground. Then, he proceeded to head in every direction except the one they led him in. Every time they came close to hemming him in, he would take off in another direction as if playing an exciting round of keep-away.

The sun was fully up now and the temperature of the summer day as well as the aggravation level of five grown men was quickly rising to the point of a simmering kettle. More than one man made mention of possible stews and a pot roast recipe that could easily rectify the problem. Although none of them had ever tasted an emu steak, they were all willing to try one.

After more than an hour of shooing, running, begging, and cursing, the bird was within inches of the interior circle. Just one more step and he'd be there. Marion was closest to the free end of the rope by this point and he gently knelt down to pick up the end without spooking the animal. The other four practiced their most soothing language of the day to try and coax the bird one step over.

It worked! The rope cinched around his foot as soon as the claw touched the ground. Marion pulled it straight up in the air putting the emu into a makeshift high kick which seemed to upset the bird a great deal. He began to hop about on his one free foot with Marion holding on as tight as possible. C.J. made for his back but missed falling head first on the other side. Jimmy and Marcus tried to get the pillowcase around his head, but the business end of a beak held them at bay.

"Grab the other foot!" Marion, who had now become the pivotal point in the makeshift emu compass, yelled in desperation.

Chris responded to his father's instructions by grabbing the meaty part of the drumstick. Jimmy saw that he was little more than a kid on a spinning top and dove in lower in the hopes of getting the fowl off balance. C.J. and Marcus pushed while Chris and Jimmy pulled. Marion just held on.

They finally had him on the ground but the bird was less than pleased. He continued to thrash about and landed a hard kick on his owner's face. When Jimmy finally emerged from the fray, he was sporting a particularly nasty gash on the left side of his lip.

Emu steaks were sounding better and better.

"Mr. Watson, what brings you into the E.R. today?" The young kid of a doctor asked in a pleasant manner.

"My lip got cut." Jimmy responded sullenly.

"How'd you cut your lip, sir?"

"Got kicked in the head by an emu."

The young doctor stopped mid exam and stared at his patient. He'd never heard that one before and he was hoping that he'd misunderstood. "You got what?"

"I got kicked in the head by an emu." Jimmy wasn't in the mood to relive the morning in great detail.

Putting his pen down, he looked over at Mr. Watson to see if he displayed any other signs of senility. "An emu?"

"Yep."

"Why exactly did an emu kick you in the face?"

"Because I was holding onto his foot." Jimmy's patience was growing thinner by the minute.

"Why did you grab his foot?"

"To get a rope around it."

The doctor picked up his pen and the chart to make notions on the record but wasn't exactly sure administration would believe the emu write up. "Mr. Watson, do you normally grab an emu's foot to put a rope around it?" He was slightly more sarcastic with his retort.

"Only when I'm trying to wrestle one into a trailer." Jimmy stated with equal vigor.

Six stitches later, Myrna drove Jimmy home where he spent the rest of the afternoon fuming about the projects he still had to get to and the wasted morning he had spent with those cotton picking birds!

ಅನ

"What smells so good?" Jimmy asked walking into the kitchen, carrying a bucketful of freshly picked peas.

"Country fried steaks." Myrna responded. She turned and looked at the peas as he poured them out onto an opened newspaper. "Got some peas?"

"Yeah. Probably won't have too many more after this. Looked like they were just about done."

"Well, the freezer's full now. I'll give some of those to the kids for them to put up."

She continued with supper while Jimmy went to wash up. When he returned, most of the food was already on the table. He fixed the drinks for both of them.

"Are these those emu steaks I brought up here?" Jimmy asked, placing a healthy piece on his plate.

"Yeah. I thought we might as well try them."

Jimmy filled his plate with the corn, beans, and a homemade biscuit while Myrna did the same. They sat in a comfortable silence.

"I think I need to sharpen these knives." Jimmy was trying to work his way through the first cut of the steak.

"Kinda hard to cut, isn't it?" Myrna agreed.

Finally, the piece was severed, but the battle had only begun. As a child, Jimmy had tried some of his uncle's homemade jerky. Having never actually tried to chew shoe leather, he could only imagine that jerky was roughly the same challenge. At least his uncle's jerky had been. Now, that experienced provided little comfort to the shoe leather he had in his mouth. Finally, after drinking a glass of tea to retain any level of moisture available, Jimmy finally won the battle.

"Is your piece tough?"

"Just like shoe leather." Myrna was still working on her piece.

"Those birds ain't good for nothing." He pushed the steak aside and dug into the vegetables.

છ૪ૐ

Myrna and Jimmy sat in the crowded lobby for more than two hours waiting to be seen. The doctor had been called into emergency surgery and the patient load was bursting when he finally began seeing his regular patients that afternoon. It made for a long day for everyone. Jimmy shifted in the chair trying to find a position that didn't pinch the disc in his back but it was no use. He wouldn't be fully comfortable until he could get up and walk around a bit. As the room began to clear out, the nurse stepped through the door and called Jimmy back to the exam room. The doctor would be in shortly.

"Hello, Mr. Watson. How are you doing today?" Dr. Masterson asked cordially.

"I'm good. How are you?" Jimmy returned his handshake.

"Mrs. Watson, how are you?" The doctor greeted Myrna in turn.

"Doing good." Myrna replied.

Dr. Masterson sat down and stared intently at the chart in his hand before turning his attention back to Jimmy.

"Mr. Watson, your test results showed something that we're very concerned about. There seems to be a mass on your liver. It looks very suspicious. I think it's going to need to come out." There was no way to soften the blow so he didn't try to. It was always best to be straightforward in these situations.

"How serious is it?" Myrna whispered.

The doctor pulled an X-ray out from an oversized envelope and secured it to a backlight. "Here is his liver," he pointed with his pen at the organ. "And here is the mass which has developed."

They stared at the white blob on the screen. It looked to be roughly the size of an orange.

"As you can see, it's a substantial size. I believe, given Jimmy's history, it needs to come out sooner rather than later."

"When will we be able to schedule the surgery?" Myrna asked while choking back some tears.

"I'll put in an order with the hospital to get the operation scheduled as soon as possible. My staff will set everything up and let you know when we have a date."

"Will he be taking the same kind of chemo this time?" Myrna knew the routine which lay ahead.

"It's really too early to tell. Once we have the mass out, I'll send it off to be biopsied. Then we'll send the results over to your oncologist," he shuffled through the chart again to verify which oncologist they were seeing. "To Dr. Kapel's office. He'll be able to recommend the best treatment for you at that time."

Jimmy watched as Myrna absorbed the news slowly. He knew the outcome wouldn't be favorable. He had known this day would come eventually.

"I'm sorry to be the bearer of such bad news," Dr. Masterson said solemnly. "We're going to get this out and go after it very aggressively."

"Thank you, doctor." Jimmy managed to say before leading Myrna out to the car.

An eerie quiet fell on the car during the ride home. A drive that normally took fifteen minutes to complete now seemed like hours. Both lost in thought. Myrna headed to the kitchen as soon as she got in the house. She had a roast cooking in the crock pot and she needed to get the rest of supper on the stove. She set a pot of tea to boil and then began rummaging around in the refrigerator for the leftover beans. No, they had finished those up yesterday. She'd need to go to the freezer and pull something from there. She made her way down the stairs, opened the door on her left, and turned toward the opposite wall to face the two large chest freezers that stood beside one another. One primarily held meat, the other vegetables although an overlap of that organizational system was known to occur depending on the space available at any given moment. She held open the top for several moments before focusing on anything inside. It was filled to capacity. Jimmy always kept them both filled. It was just the way he was, the way he'd always been. Something she'd taken for granted all this time. And now, as she stared down at the fruits of his labor, she began to wonder what her world would be like if she lost him. For the first time since she heard the news, she allowed herself to cry.

Chapter Eight

JIMMY LOADED UP several bales of hay onto the trailer and drove out to feed the cows. Outwardly he felt fine. Hadn't even had a cold this winter. Inwardly, his body was turning against him. He couldn't feel the tumor. There was no sign it existed, yet the doctor said it was there and needed to come out. Jimmy knew the doctor was right. He saw the X-rays with his own eyes. And this time, it was much bigger than before.

He thought about his life and the plans he put in place over the last few years. Those arrangements should see Myrna through if

143

anything happened. When it happened. Financially, she should be okay.

He cut the twine on the bale with his pocket knife and spread the hay around. That way the smaller animals could eat without being pushed out by the larger members of the herd. It wasn't hard to take care of a bunch of cows. For the most part, they took care of themselves. But they did need to be fed and watered daily. Hay had to be purchased, loaded, unloaded, and stored. Then, they eventually had to be taken to the market. That could be a challenge if they didn't want to go in the cattle trailer. And what if they got sick? Things could get complicated very quickly if one of them fell ill.

What would Myrna do if he wasn't around? They'd always worked well as a team. He handled his part. She handled hers. Each worked well by not encroaching on the other. Now the possibility loomed overhead that their carefully working system may not last much longer.

He looked out over the pasture. The pecan trees he planted when they first moved out here were mature now. Each year those trees made enough to keep the entire family in a continuous supply. But he also knew those trees required maintenance as well. He fertilized them every year. He pruned off the rotten or broken limbs. He gathered the harvest when it fell. Not hard or overwhelming work but another weight his wife would have to bear when he was gone.

He wanted her to enjoy her golden years not work her fingers to the bone trying to keep the life they had together. He knew his boys would help out when they could but they had their own lives to lead. They couldn't spend all their time leading the life of their father. Their families needed them. He couldn't burden them anymore than he could burden his wife. Something would have to go.

⊗⊗

After several sessions of spirited debate, the council decided to heed Jimmy's advice and build the new sanctuary before inflation drove the prices higher. They felt certain they could raise at least half the required funds. They set the goal to be raised initially at sixty percent of the cost which would still be a reasonable amount but would reduce the length of the loan by more than five years. It was the only way Horace would agree albeit reluctantly.

Abigail's one stipulation was to ask Jimmy to work closely with the project. He was the only person with experience in building and he knew far more than anyone what was needed and what could be omitted. She felt certain if he was directly involved from the beginning, everything would be okay. She was stunned when he agreed but told her that his time would be limited.

"Jimmy, I had no idea."

"We only found out yesterday. It kinda caught us by surprise." He replied quietly.

"How are you feeling?"

"I'm feeling fine. I had no idea. They found it during my checkup."

"How's Myrna doing with all this?" Abigail knew she'd be beside herself with worry if it had been her husband, Tom.

"She's doing okay. I'll have her call you when she gets home. She's at the grocery store."

⚛

The waiting room held an unnatural sense of déjà vu for the family as they waited to hear about Jimmy. Myrna was far more fidgety than normal. She obviously remembered the last time Jimmy had major surgery. Dr. Masterson had reassured her that a different type of anesthesia was being used but that didn't stop her from cornering the anesthesiologist before surgery and reiterating her concern. Now, there was nothing she could do. Her husband's life was in the hands of the doctors and the good Lord.

Dr. Masterson came out much sooner than expected. Only an hour had passed. The surgery should have taken two full hours at least. The growth was easier to get to than they expected. It wasn't inside the liver. It was attached to the outside. Its placement made it simple to remove.

"So what's the bad news?" Dylan asked as he watched the doctor's grim expression.

"It wasn't the only one. We found dozens of small growths. We removed all we could see but there may be more which were so small we couldn't find them. There was simply no way to get all the tumors out."

It was the first time Myrna forgot how to breathe.

෩

"I don't want to move." Myrna began clearing the dishes from the table with gusto.

Jimmy watched her. He knew this decision would take some convincing but he'd thought of little else since the doctor explained the dire outcome of the surgery. He simply couldn't leave his wife with so much to take care of in her golden years.

"This isn't going to be like the last time." He said quietly.

Myrna glared at him. "We're going to fight this. You have an appointment with Dr. Kapel tomorrow." She picked up the bowl of soup and returned to the kitchen leaving him for a moment.

He sat at the table patiently waiting her return. "I know I have that appointment tomorrow and we'll see what he says but there are no guarantees with this thing. I want you to think about it. If something happens to me, I don't want you to have to worry about taking care of all this." His calm was startling and in sharp contrast to the angst she felt so deeply.

"I don't want to move, Jimmy." The topic was closed for further discussion.

Dr. Kapel offered less hope than Myrna would have liked. He confirmed Jimmy's worst suspicions. The biopsy report and Dr. Masterson's notes indicated a very aggressive strain of malignancy. The chemo would need to be far more intense than before and even so, there were no guarantees it would be successful.

"With an aggressive treatment, we're only looking at another two years under the most optimistic circumstances." He gave them a moment to absorb the information.

"I'm very sorry." He continued solemnly.

148

Myrna cleared her throat. "Isn't there anything else that can be done?"

"There are new trials that come out every day. I'll submit your name for those but I have no way of knowing if or when you might get accepted. Even if you do get accepted to one, I couldn't begin to fathom what the outcome might be for an untested treatment program. With the options we have today, that's the best possible outcome I can see."

"How long would I have if I don't take the treatments?" Jimmy whispered.

Myrna glared at him in stunned silence. There was never a question that he wouldn't go forward with the treatment. Not in her mind. They were going to fight this. He was going to get well again.

"There's no way to know the answer to that. The time would be greatly reduced certainly. Perhaps only six months." Dr. Kapel responded.

Jimmy nodded, lost in contemplation.

"I wouldn't recommend skipping these treatments. I know they will be difficult but they have been proven to increase the life expectancy. I don't want to give you false hope, but we can offer you a viable treatment program that will give you longer with your family."

Again, Jimmy nodded. Myrna studied him closely. She could see the wheels turning in his mind and wondered exactly what he was thinking about.

"Then let's set up the treatments." Jimmy relented.

The nurse provided them with all the necessary paperwork a few minutes later. A new port would be inserted. The receptionist was making that appointment at the hospital now. Once the port was in and healed, blood work would be drawn with the initial treatment following quickly afterward. This round of chemo included five separate drugs each designed to target the aggressive strain Jimmy was fighting. It would be more difficult than before and he may experience symptoms more severely. After six treatments they would conduct another CAT scan and adjust the treatment from there. It was the best they could do.

Jimmy didn't mention the idea of moving at supper that night. He didn't mention it the following day either. Myrna needed some time to process the information. She had not come to terms with the idea that he would die. She still wanted to believe that they had many more years together. Maybe they would, but that prospect looked bleak. He knew the discussion couldn't wait much longer.

"I'm not ready to talk about that Jimmy." Myrna retorted, clearly aggravated that this topic was being brought up again in the middle of everything they had to deal with.

"I know." It had been three days since they visited Dr. Kapel. Jimmy's appointment to insert the port was scheduled for tomorrow morning.

Myrna sat silently staring at the television.

"We need to start thinking about your future." He continued calmly.

"My future involves getting you well again." Her arms folded in a dangerous way.

Jimmy shifted slightly in his chair. "You heard what the doctor said. I don't have very much longer. We need to make sure that you're taken care of once I'm gone."

"We set up the will and everything years ago. I'll be fine." Myrna huffed. "And you're not going to die."

"But what if I do?"

The reality proved too painful to think about. "You're not going to die." She avowed firmly before heading into the kitchen to bake a cobbler.

CR&O

Robby knew all the architects in the area. Lowenstein and Sons was the most reasonably priced. They also offered discounted service fees for charity organizations. It helped ensure their firm always had a waiting list of projects to complete. It took eight weeks to get the official designs for the sanctuary back. Jimmy looked them over thoroughly before submitting a copy to the county for the building permit.

He had agreed to act as the contractor for the project. It would be an extensive project but it would also save the church almost twenty percent over hiring a general contractor. Besides, with the exception of a few contractors in the area, he knew more about the business than the vast majority of new contractors popping up here and there. Robby could help him out on some of the issues. He'd hire out the rest. Staying busy would be the best tonic for his upcoming treatments.

Over the next few days, the thoughts of building plans and church additions were driven out of his mind by the sheer violence of the drugs coursing through his body. The first bout of chemo had nothing on this round. His treatment session was four days long for an hour each day. After the first day, he felt as though he'd been slammed against a brick wall. The second day, the thought of food turned his stomach. By the third day, he was unable to hold anything solid down. The fourth day actually proved to be the least devastating, probably because his body had nothing left to offer.

It took an entire week to recover, if you could call it recovering. He felt better, far from great mind you, but good enough to start making preparations for the groundbreaking. He reviewed the estimates from the roofer and the electrician. They could start as soon as Robby poured the foundation and got the frame up. That project should come along nicely.

Knowing that the church project was headed in the right direction freed his mind to focus on the other major concern he'd been pondering. Myrna. She refused to think about the possibility of moving, let alone hear any arguments he used to try to convince her. She held firmly to the notion that this was her home and he would make it through this battle alive. If the first round of chemo proved anything to him, it was that he was very clearly closer to the end of life than the beginning. He had to figure out a way to change her mind.

"How are you feeling?" She asked for the tenth time that day as he sat down for supper.

"I'm alright, I guess. I just don't feel like doing anything. I'm completely wiped out." He had no appetite despite the mountain of food before him.

"You need to take it easy." She soothed.

"I can't take it easy. I've got to go down after supper and take care of the cows." He reminded her, a not so subtle introduction to the conversation ahead.

"I'll go down there and take care of them. You rest."

"We need to seriously think about getting rid of them and getting you in a smaller place that will be easier to manage."

Her lips pursed. "I don't want to move, Jimmy."

"You're not going to be able to take care of this house, the cows, the farm, all this land, and me. You're going to run yourself ragged." He had to make her see.

"What about you? You're going through these treatments and trying to build a new sanctuary for the church. You should be focusing on getting well." She countered with spirit.

"I'm not going to get well." It was the first time he'd voiced his belief aloud.

She huffed deeply, willing the tears to remain at bay. "Yes, you are." She got up quickly and left the table.

A few minutes later, she returned wearing her straw hat that she wore while she gardened.

154

"Where are you going?" He asked, stunned.

"I'm going to take care of the cows." And she was gone.

৫৪৯

"I don't know how you do everything, Jimmy." Abigail said, shaking her head.

He was wearing a jacket despite the rising temperature outside. His body ravaged by the fourth round of chemo. Not for the first time, she had asked him to step down and let someone else oversee the project. They may not have as much experience but they could learn. It was better than him trying to kill himself when he clearly needed to rest.

"You just have to keep moving." He replied.

"If it were me, I'd be in the bed resting." She knew Myrna tried to get him to rest to no avail.

"I might wear out but I won't rust out." He declared firmly. Then he excused himself and went to greet the county inspector.

৫৪৯

"Your Daddy wants to sell the house and move me into a smaller place." Myrna told

Emma as they walked around the pasture for her evening constitutional.

It was a shock to Emma's system. "Move?"

"Yeah."

"Why does he want you to do that?" Emma had never considered that to be even a remote possibility.

"He's worried about me having to take care of all this if anything happens to him." Myrna seemed far away.

Emma let the statement sink in. "Do you want to move?"

"No."

"Then tell him you don't want to." Emma knew it was bad advice before the words were out of her mouth.

"I have but he's pretty determined." Myrna stopped and looked out over the pasture which was sprouting a beautiful green layer of grass for the cows to graze on."

Emma watched her for a long time.

"He's right. He does most of the work around here. It's about to kill me with just him being sick. I can't take care of everything by myself." She wiped a tear away. "I never thought I'd have to."

Myrna took a deep breath and continued walking leaving Emma to pick up the pieces of her broken heart.

156

CRED

When Jimmy stood on the scale after the sixth treatment, he was thirty pounds lighter than before his surgery. He was surprised he hadn't lost more weight seeing as he hadn't eaten a good hearty meal in over four months. Now, they sat and waited for Dr. Kapel to tell them whether their efforts were fruitful or all for naught.

The verdict was a mixture. The tumors were still present and growing. They could clearly be seen on the CAT scans. Dr. Kapel admitted that was an alarming development. On the bright side, he felt certain that they were growing slower than they would have without the treatment. He suggested four more rounds adding an additional medication which may help slow the progress even further. It was a new drug, only available in the last month, but it showed promising results.

Jimmy was uncertain. "How much worse will this treatment be?"

"It's a very harsh drug. Most patients experience some rough symptoms with it," Dr. Kapel confirmed Jimmy's suspicions. "We'll try to keep the dosage somewhere in the middle range to balance out the positive effects without maximizing the harsh side effects."

Jimmy looked over at Myrna.

"What's the likelihood that this new drug will help?" She whispered.

"There are no guarantees. It's showing about a fifty percent improvement in most studies."

"But it won't stop it completely?" She pressed.

"No." Dr. Kapel shook his head. "No, there is nothing on the market today that will completely reverse the growth that Jimmy has."

"How much time will it give me if it does work?" Jimmy stared at the floor not wanting to see Myrna's face in pain.

"Maybe a couple of months. There's really no way to tell."

"So I'll just be living to take the chemo at that point?"

Dr. Kapel had no answer for that. He was sworn to save lives and everything he knew about medicine told him that this drug would prolong Jimmy's life. But at what cost? It was a decision only Jimmy could make.

"Let us talk about it." Jimmy nodded to the doctor.

"Do you want to go home and discuss it and call the office with your answer tomorrow?" Dr. Kapel understood the magnitude of what they were facing.

"Yeah." Jimmy replied.

The trip home was quiet. When they pulled into the carport, Jimmy turned off the car and looked over at Myrna. She hadn't moved during the entire ride.

"I don't want to take those treatments. I love you but I don't want to go through that. I'm not going to be here much longer. I want to sell this place and get you in a more manageable home." He was firm.

Myrna swallowed hard. "Will it make you feel better?"

"Yes. I don't want to die worrying about you."

"Okay. Let's look for a place tomorrow." She wiped the tears away as she opened the door and headed in the house.

Chapter Nine

SHOPPING FOR A new house was the last thing Myrna wanted to do as they set out in search of the new home Jimmy insisted on. She didn't like the cookie cutter designed McMassions that dotted the landscape in nearby Warner Robins. She didn't like the smaller homes. It's difficult to find what you want when you really don't know what you're looking for. Or when you don't want to look in the first place.

Cost was not an issue to Jimmy. He knew they would pay the new place off when they sold the farm. She should even have some

161

money left over to help see her through any difficulty that may arise. He did, however, look at any home she showed the slightest interest in with a detailed eye. He wasn't about to put her in anything less than she deserved.

The houses she liked were few and far between. Either the houses were too big and the yards too small or the floor plan was cumbersome and unwieldy. Some had ten foot ceilings with massive chandlers. She would never be able to reach that to dust and clean. She didn't need five bedrooms and four baths. She didn't need an office and a study. She needed a functional home designed for an older woman who would soon be a widow. Apparently, that wasn't a popular demographic on the market.

They looked for three weeks. Jimmy prodding her onward with each step. He was on a mission and wouldn't be deterred. She was beginning to wish she'd never agreed to this fool-hearty notion.

"There's one other option we haven't thought about yet." He mentioned as they ate lunch at the Cracker Barrel. They were scheduled to meet an agent at a local open house within the hour.

"What's that?" She sipped her water while finishing up the pork chop.

"We still have that last lot that never sold. I could design you the exact house you want and build it for you." He watched her reaction.

A thousand thoughts flooded her mind. "Jimmy, you're sick. You're already trying to finish up the church project. You don't need to try to take on something else."

"It wouldn't be that hard. I could have everything finished in six months or so." He sipped his sweet tea.

"But. . ." She couldn't form the words. She couldn't wrap her mind around the fact that he might not be here in six months.

He read her mind. "I'll have time to finish it."

"I don't know." She stammered.

"Let's see what this guy shows us and then we'll decide. You've looked at everything else and haven't liked anything. There's not much left on the market that we haven't tried. The only thing left to do is to build." He was ever the realist.

"We'll see."

The open house offered more of the same. These homes were nice but top heavy. Each home sat on a third of an acre. She didn't want a lot of land but she did want to be able to walk outside without hearing her neighbors sneeze in their kitchen. This neighborhood made her feel claustrophobic and trapped. She could not see herself living there.

After supper, Jimmy went to his office. He came back two hours later with a rough draft. Three bedrooms, two baths, a large kitchen with a breakfast nook, a formal dining room for family get-togethers, and a sunroom which would get plenty of light for her sewing. The lot was slopped so a basement had been added for extra storage and the possibility of an extra bedroom if needed. It had a two car garage and plenty of room without being overbearing.

She studied the sketch before looking up at him. "Yeah, that's what I want."

"Okay. I'll get started on it tomorrow."

CRBO

For Jimmy, working on a deadline was nothing new. He'd done it all his life. Now, time became a commodity more precious than gold. Lowenstein wouldn't be able to look at the sketches for almost a month. It would take an additional three weeks to draw up the blueprints. That would greatly cut into an already tight schedule. Another architect was found who was equally skilled but double the price. He finished the plans in less than two weeks.

Robby brought his backhoe to the lot early Saturday morning. Dylan was already there with his chainsaw and splitter. He figured to kill two birds in the process by preparing his woodpile for next winter. Jake and Heath would be able to help while Robby cleared the stumps away. Jimmy drove his tractor over. Jimmy wanted the house to face the morning sun. It meant taking down two extra trees but it saved the old chimney and the area surrounding it.

"You want me to knock that down, too?" Robby asked once the main area was cleared.

"No. I got something planned for that."

Robby and Dylan looked at the stack of bricks. It was roughly four feet tall and a waste of space as far as they were concerned.

"What are you going to do with it, Dad?" Dylan wanted to know.

"I'm going to fix it up like one of those old timey wells with a pulley and a bucket. Then your mama can plant some flowers around it for decoration."

The boys looked at it again.

"Maybe fix up a little bird bath in the middle of it." Jimmy continued. "Your mama would like that."

Their dad was the only one who would have seen that in an old pile of rubble but looking at it now through his eyes, they could see it as well. Their mother would definitely like that.

Robby pointed to the giant mulberry tree nearby. "You ought to put a bench or something under that tree so she can sit out here and enjoy it."

"Yeah, I'm planning on it."

Working on both projects simultaneously worked to Jimmy's advantage. He was able to use most of the same contractors for the house that he used for the new sanctuary. They were a good team of professionals. Robby and Dylan lent their talents as well but their schedules were limited by work and family. On the other hand, Heath and Jake spent most of their afternoons working with their granddad to finish up the house he insisted on building from scratch.

Jimmy refused to shudder away from any issue that needed tending although he was becoming a little slower in his movements. It had been six weeks since he told Dr. Kapel that he wouldn't be taking any further treatment. Six weeks since he'd convinced Myrna that he needed to do this to pass peacefully. Six weeks since he'd assured her that he could finish this one last project for her.

Things were progressing but not as quickly as he would have hoped. All the underground pipes were in. The foundation and framing was up. The masons were finishing up with the front half of the house. That left the back and the basement to finish which was considerably larger by comparison. They would need at least another week to brick the entire house. The roofers were putting the shingles on this week. Now all he had to do was to wait for the inspector to come out and okay the electrical work and he could begin to install the sheetrock. He was already a day late. It was putting Jimmy further behind by the minute.

The sanctuary was in much the same boat. They had a significant head start on that project. All the exterior work was completed. Now they were working on the interior portion which provided its own challenges. The wrong pipes had initially been installed for the baptismal basin. Those had to be removed and replaced before any additional work in that area could continue. It had taken two weeks to correct the issue.

Jimmy looked at his watch for the fifth time that morning. He didn't have time to wait on the inspector. Nor did he have time to wait around while these people figured out which pipe to install. They should have known that from the beginning. He was on a schedule. A very tight schedule. And there was no way to push this deadline back any further.

☙❧

"It's hard to believe you're moving out of this house." Shannon said with a touch of melancholy. The girls had come over to help their mom sort through some of the things in the house. After almost twenty-five years in the same place, stuff seemed to hide in every tiny crevice. As they packed the third box, they realized things were, in fact, multiplying at a rapid rate. Where did it all come from?

Emma pulled out a shoebox filled with treasures from her high school days. She roared with laughter across the room.

"Shannon, do you remember this?" She squealed, holding up a photo album from the last trip they took together with the church youth group shortly before she left for college and a new life.

Shannon joined her sister as they sat on the bed and laughed at long forgotten photos. They began to dig through the box together. There were notes from Emma's high school sweetheart dealing a secret rendezvous that Myrna was intrigued to learn about. She found a homemade pendant soliciting votes for her best friend's homecoming bid. Emma didn't remember why she'd kept an old matchbook from Salty Dave's Crab Shack until she opened the packet and saw the name Mitch and a phone number jotted on the inside. It was another adventure Myrna was only now learning about.

"I had forgotten all about this stuff." Emma grinned.

"That's all yours so you can take it home with you." Myrna was quickly losing her attachment to different possessions.

"Oh, I'm definitely keeping this box." Emma made a stack of things to take home with her.

"This was y'all's room so anything you want you both need to take with you today. I don't want to move anything I don't have to."

Shannon dug further in the closet, behind some horribly outdated clothes to see what else was hidden on the shelf. "We'll get everything we want. But what do you want to do with anything that's left?"

"We're giving it to Goodwill." Myrna said flatly. "I've already taken over three loads. "What I don't keep and the family doesn't want is going to be given away."

"In that case, I guess we need to start a pile for donations too." Emma looked around at clothes they would never wear again. Somebody out there surely wanted a Member's Only jacket. Nobody in this room wanted it, but there had to be someone out there who desperately wanted such an item.

Myrna wasn't the only one who'd begun the overwhelming task of decluttering. When Jimmy wasn't at the new house or the church, he was down in the barn or in the basement sorting through mountains of treasures of his own. He'd filled up the truck with a dozen old motors that he'd meant to fix one day. There wouldn't be time for that now. He hauled those off to the scrap metal yard. He'd taken a load of cows to the market. It would take at least another three trips before they were all gone. He was trying to time it so that all the hay was gone at about the same time as the cows. That way he wouldn't be stuck with a mountain of hay to get rid of. Horace liked to do a lot of woodwork and projects around the house. Jimmy gave him all the old scrap lumber he had laying around. He'd also started dividing up his tools between Robby and Dylan. They would be able to get a lot of use out of those.

⋘⋙

Bill listed the farm a month later. He needed to give Myrna and Jimmy a chance to get the home staged for a proper showing. Even still, market interest wasn't what he hoped it would be. Families today didn't want the responsibility of so much property. They were moving away from the country and into more urban areas. It would take some time to find the right buyer.

For Jimmy, that was the wrong answer. He knew Bill wouldn't steer him wrong and he knew that if anything ever happened to him, Bill would make sure that Myrna got fair value for the sale. But that didn't negate the need for him to see her safely in another home where she could spend the rest of her days without worry. This place had to go. It was the only way the equation would balance in his mind.

೮ఠಿಠ

"I'm afraid the tumors are getting bigger. There's a marked increase in size since you were in her three months ago." Dr. Kapel told him gravely.

Jimmy nodded. He knew they had grown. He could feel them pressing against his stomach and kidneys. He felt constantly full regardless of how much or how little he ate. He winched as the doctor pressed on his abdomen to complete the exam.

"Are you in any pain?" He asked his patient.

"Yeah. It's starting to bother me a good bit." Jimmy was honest.

A prescription was written for oxycodone. "I'd like to see you again next month."

Jimmy looked at him quizzically.

"I want to make sure that we're managing your pain as well as we can. You shouldn't have to hurt through this."

"Okay."

CS80

The workers finished with the drywall in good time. He was starting to feel more comfortable about finishing the house on schedule. Then the rains came and prevented the concrete company from pouring the driveway. Things were pretty well saturated. It would take at least a week before everything was dry enough to pour, once the rains stopped and the sun came out. Sadly, the forecasts called for heavy rain showers for the next five days.

The steeple for the church arrived during the worst of the flood. One of the final steps before the open house and it, too, was held up by the weather. Jimmy couldn't get the crane scheduled fast enough once the sun finally broke through for good. Shannon and little Katie drove over for the big event. About half the members were there. Like a candle on a birthday cake, this steeple represented the beginning of a new journey and a time for celebration. For Jimmy, it came with a sigh of relief. Now, there were only two things left to do. He had to focus on finishing the new home and selling the old house.

Katie hugged her grandpa as he talked to the crane operator and the men who had come by to help steady the placement. She loved the idea of her own private playhouse, complete with its own tower. She crawled through the door on the side and opened the slat window.

"Come on, Katie. You have to get out of there." Shannon coaxed her to move.

"But I'm playing castles." Katie didn't understand what all the fuss was about but she hoped her mom would bring this playhouse home with them.

"Sweetie, you've got to move. They're about to lift the steeple with the crane." Shannon was firm.

Convinced that her wish was coming true, Katie tumbled out of the window landing head first with the bouncy grace of a second grader. She was none too happy to learn that the crane was not actually putting the playhouse into her mom's car but it was putting it on top of the building. Who needed a playhouse on a big ol' building? Then she saw grandpa stick his head out of the side window she'd just tumbled out of. She didn't understand why he wanted it up there. And the only explanation she got was that's where a steeple goes. Adults could be really weird sometimes.

CRRO

The house was ready to move into a month later. There were still some things that needed to be done. None of the landscaping had been started. The yard was a bare mound of red clay. Jimmy had ordered several trailers of sod to be delivered and installed but that wouldn't arrive for another week, when the sod farm held the next cutting. He wasn't willing to hold up the move waiting on grass to grow.

They began transferring boxes of miscellaneous things first. Truckload after truckload ferried the three mile trek. The main moving party was scheduled for that weekend when everyone had off from work. Until then, Myrna wanted to get a jump on organizing her new abode. Even with all the cleaning and donations, she was still amazed at how much stuff remained to be transferred. She made a mental resolution to get rid of most of that junk when she had the time. It was one of many things she wanted to do.

With all the furniture and heavy items moved, it seemed strange to walk through her empty home after so many years there. She ran her hand along the countertop where she'd stood and fixed thousands of meals. She walked through the dining room where Jimmy had painstakingly installed the crown molding that she saw in a magazine and loved. She paused in her old bedroom where she and Jimmy had spent so many hours discussing problems and future plans. This was more than a house. It was a home. It was their home. They'd built it together. Now, she was moving into her home. The house she would live in alone until her end came. She'd known this day was coming, but somehow she'd always been able to push it off into the future. Now, a part of her life was clearly at an end. She took a deep breath, wiped the tears from her cheek, and picked up the last box before closing that chapter of her life.

⊗⊗

Bill brought the paperwork over for Jimmy and Myrna to review. It was only the second offer they'd had on the old place. It wasn't what they were hoping to get but it wasn't an insult either. He watched his friend peruse through the figures.

"You're going to need some time to go over it." Bill said.

"No, I'm going to make a counter offer but then when they come back, I'm going to take it." Jimmy winced. The pain medicine offered little relief despite the dosage having been increased twice already.

"That won't be up to the list price." Bill wanted to make sure his friend knew that he was likely to lose some money on the deal.

"You know, you don't have to push this sell through. You can wait until someone is willing to pay more."

"I don't have time to wait." Jimmy was determined.

Bill sighed. "I know, but you know that I wouldn't let anything happen to Myrna. I'd make sure she got a good deal and a fair price for everything."

"I know you would, but I don't want her to have to worry about any of this once I'm gone. I want to know she's settled and taken care of."

As Bill drove away that afternoon, he said a silent prayer that he would be strong enough to meet death with as much grace as his friend.

CRSSO

Robby reviewed the closing paperwork with his mom as Bill explained each section. The couple buying the farm reminded her so much of her family thirty years earlier. Their

176

kids were grown and freshly out of the house. They were nearing retirement. And they yearned for life in the country. Just like she and Jimmy once had. It seemed strange to sell their home without him while he was still alive. He didn't have the strength to sit through any of this but he was still alive. It was still their home, the home they'd built together through blood, sweat, and tears.

She forced those thoughts from her mind and focused once again on the numbers in front of her. She was sure they were right but Robby had taken out his pocket calculator and added everything one more time. Just like Jimmy would do.

After an hour of signing a book of papers, she and Robby left the lawyer's office with the certified check in hand.

"Are you okay?" Robby asked putting his hand out to help her step off the curve.

"Yeah, I'm okay." She mumbled. Jimmy would be relieved that everything was finalized and she was taken care of. It would help him rest easy. She had a home to see her through the rest of her days. She would survive.

"You sure?" Robby prodded.

Myrna nodded. "I'm just glad this part is over."

He seemed to understand. "Me, too."

Jimmy was asleep when she came home. He looked so pale and feeble in such a large bed. She went to the kitchen to start supper. When she checked on him a short time later, he was lying awake, looking out the bedroom door.

"How did it go?" He asked as soon as the door framed her silhouette.

"Everything went fine. All the paperwork is signed and the check is in the bank." She said soothingly.

"Did Robby go over the numbers before you signed the contract?" He had to be sure.

"Yes. All the numbers were right." She sat beside him and lifted the straw in the glass of ginger ale to his mouth. He lifted his head slightly and sipped before the exhaustion of such a simple act overtook him and he collapsed back on his pillow.

She stayed by his side stroking his head until the timer on the stove went off. "Do you want anything to eat?" She whispered.

"No."

"Okay."

The next two days passed quietly. Robby and Dylan took turns sitting with their father in the afternoons. Emma and Shannon called and made plans to visit on the weekend. Jimmy could no longer sit in his favorite recliner. There was no more energy left in his body. He relegated all movement to necessary trips to the bathroom, returning to bed completely spent by the process. Myrna stayed by his side the entire time.

By Thursday, his breathing was shallow and labored. Myrna dipped a piece of crushed ice into his mouth to ease the soreness. The pain medicine caused him to drift in and out of sleep.

"Do you want some more ice?" She whispered as his eyes flickered open.

He shook his head, then said goodbye for the last time.

Chapter Ten

"ROBBY," MYRNA TOOK a deep breath.
"What's wrong, Mama?"
"Your daddy's gone home, son."
"I'll be right there."

Emma took Robby's call far more calmly than she would have imagined. Of course, she'd had a year of tears to help prepare for this moment. Now there were a million things that needed to be done. She had to call her kids, notify work, and pack some clothes. She knew she should have put together a bag just in case, but that seemed to be inviting trouble, accepting the inevitable. It was giving up hope. Now she second guessed that decision as she frantically raced to get everything done and get to her family as quickly as possible.

Amy walked out to the garage where Dylan was hunched over his latest restoration project desperately in search of a bolt that was playing hide and seek behind the radiator. When he saw her face, he instantly knew the worst.

"What's wrong?"

"You need to get over to your mom's house." She wiped away a fresh stream of tears.

"Daddy?"

She began to sob openly and nodded. "A few minutes ago. Robby just called."

He nodded, hugged his wife tightly, and went to take a quick shower.

Shannon heard the phone ring as she shut the door to Katie's room. The child had suddenly developed an intense fear of goblins thanks in part to some troublesome kids at school. More than one story and a hefty amount of patience had been needed to get her to bed.

"It's for you. It's Robby." Darren said handing her the phone.

She didn't need to hear him tell her to come to their mother's home. She didn't need to hear the pain in his voice as he choked back the tears. She didn't need to hear that their father had gone peacefully. Somehow she knew. She had felt the emptiness as soon as Darren handed her the phone.

"When?" Darren heard her say.

A pause.

"How's Mom?"

Another pause.

"I'll be there as fast as I can."

She pressed 'end' on the receiver and turned to tell Darren the news. Before she could take one step, she hit the floor, as surely as if a mule had planted his feet in her stomach. She couldn't breathe. She couldn't speak. All she could do was weep.

⊂℘℈⊃

Robby was the first to arrive, followed shortly by Emma and Dylan. Shannon lived further away and would be there within the hour. The hospice nurse was sitting with his mother offering comfort and companionship. They said nothing of significance but then what could be said?

After hugging his mom for a long time, he left the two ladies chatting in the living room and went to see his dad. Dad could have been sleeping. Robby had watched him sleeping for years in that same position in front of the television. He felt an arm slide around his waist and turned to find his oldest sister wiping away tears.

"He looks so peaceful." She whispered.

"Yeah, he does. Like he just drifted off to sleep." Robby agreed.

"At least he's out of pain."

"Yeah." Robby nodded in his customary, deliberate manner.

They stood there for a little while longer, absorbing the moment and the sorrow that filled the room. It soon became overwhelming so they rejoined their mother and the hospice nurse who were now in the kitchen making some coffee for the family members who would soon be arriving.

"Shannon called while I was driving over here. She said traffic was light so she should be here in about forty-five minutes." Robby informed his mother.

"I didn't call anyone else. We need to let the rest of the family know and call the preacher." Activity had helped Myrna refocus although she'd forgotten to add the basket cover to the percolator. Realizing her mistake, she poured the pot out and started again.

184

"I called Warren. He was going to let the rest of the family know but I only had the church number. I didn't have Phillip's home number. I figured you had that here."

Myrna finished making the second pot of coffee and went to the pile of papers she kept by the phone on the kitchen counter. Eventually, she found the correct piece of scrap paper with the name Phillip Edwards and a neatly written ten digit number. Robby picked up the phone to inform her minister of the news. He noticed Dylan come in and make his way around to everyone before slipping back to see their father. Phillip would begin calling church members and be there as quickly as he could.

It was after ten o'clock when Shannon walked through the door. She settled in with her family for a few minutes, then she too went for one last visit with her dad. Amid the sorrow, she felt a peace and calmness surround the house. Perhaps that was what came from growing up in such a naturally stoic family. When tragedy strikes, band together and remain calm. Somehow the darkness will always pass. Yet never before could she remember darkness quite as painful as this. She hoped she'd never face another period as bleak again.

Warren, Ruth, and Matthew pulled into the drive as the hearse from Braxton's Funeral Home arrived. The siblings filed in to say good bye to their brother while Robby and Dylan talked with Mr. Braxton and his son. The Braxton's were born to offer comfort to the grieving. Running the only funeral parlor in the county, they knew everyone and set about their work with well practiced efficiency without intrusion upon the family. They patiently waited while everyone filed into the bedroom for one last farewell before taking Jimmy away to prepare his body for the final journey. Phillip offered a prayer with the family and Jimmy drove away from home for good.

CRRO

The soul may be hungry for comfort but Southern Baptists believe the stomach should never lack nourishment. Food began arriving the next morning complete with a committee of women from the church to ensure that no one who entered left at the same weight as they arrived. Hams, casseroles, vegetables, rolls, and chicken prepared in every imaginable fashion filled the kitchen and formal dining room of Myrna's home. Paper plates, napkins, and plastic cups magically appeared filled to capacity with meals for anyone who happened to pass by.

Shannon was intrigued to find the committee huddled around the microwave as she ventured in the kitchen for a glass of tea.

"I don't know how to work this." Miss Mary was dumbfounded.

"Did you hit the button?" Patty asked.

"I hit the start button but it didn't turn on." Miss Mary pounded the button again.

"Well, it's got two knobs on it. Maybe you need to move one of them around for it to work." Susan chimed in.

"I did that." Miss Mary said in a bit of a huff. "I turned it to the one and hit start. See." She pushed the green button with vigor. "Nothing."

Shannon had to laugh. "Y'all need some help?"

The committee turned in unison. "Does this thing work?" Patty wanted clarification.

"Yeah, it works real good." Shannon couldn't contain the smile as she joined them to examine the ancient piece of machinery.

"Well, you're going to have to show us how to operate this thing." Miss Mary was beside herself. Never before had the committee's well-oiled condolence operations been interrupted by a microwave.

"You just spin this bottom knob around to about thirty and hit start." Shannon demonstrated, pressing the green button, and finally bringing the creature to life.

"But you just set the timer for thirty minutes." Patty suddenly saw hours of food ruined by over nuking.

"When it gets done, just hit the 'stop' button." Again Shannon demonstrated.

"You just set the timer for thirty minutes and that's going to overcook those peas." Patty was adamant.

"Then don't leave them in there for thirty minutes." Shannon said matter-of-factly.

"What about the timer?" Miss Mary was still befuddled.

"Oh, that timer hasn't worked in years. We never use that." Shannon clarified.

"So you just turn it on and off when you want to. How do you know when it's done?" Susan wanted to know.

"With this one, you just know." Shannon offered sagely. "Or you keep guessing until it gets warm."

"I have never seen a microwave like this before. Mine has a timer on it that you program and it stops on its own." Patty was uncertain about this contraption.

Shannon gave the familiar Watson family nod. "Yeah, Daddy got that for Mama one year for Christmas. It's one of the original Radaranges. I must have been about four or five years old." Shannon thought for a second. "It must have been around '75 or '76."

"You mean that thing is over thirty years old?" Patty was astounded.

"Yep."

"Y'all should buy your mom a new one." Miss Mary offered a stern suggestion.

"Emma and I tried to a few years ago. Mama got plumb mad at us for trying to get rid of her microwave." Shannon shuddered at the memory.

"That's because it still works." Myrna walked in to find too much criticism of beloved appliance.

Shannon decided her talents were best suited helping her sister in whatever endeavor Emma was involved in and quickly left the women to fully debate the usefulness of a thirty year old microwave. Both sisters laughed as Shannon recounted the story.

The next few days followed in a progression of food, fellowship, and fantastic stories. Everyone it seemed had something to share. Myrna and the children were unaware, although not entirely surprised, at the level of planning which had already been done for the service. When they went to Braxton's Funeral

189

Home in Byron to meet with Nora Braxton, she simply shuffled through her files until she found her information on Jimmy and pulled out a neatly handwritten sheet of paper with all his instructions for the funeral. All they had to do now was to write the obituary and choose the casket. Even in death, Jimmy wanted to make things as easy as possible for Myrna.

The congregation was seated as the family members filed down the center aisle. Myrna flanked on either side by Robby and Shannon. Dylan and Emma following close behind. Shannon had never known a longer trek in her life. Someone, it seemed, had played a terrible joke on the family and moved the front pew miles away. That was the only explanation for such a short journey to take so very long.

When they finally reached their seat, Myrna paused one last time to touch the coffin. Then she followed Emma and Dylan down the pew leaving room for Shannon and Robby. Shannon didn't recognize the hymn. She was sure she'd heard it before. It seemed to be an old standard from her youth but she couldn't be sure. All she could focus on was her mother's hand which she held and stroked. She hadn't noticed the lines there before. When had her mom aged so? When had they all? Cancer surely is a terrible bastard, aging not just the patient but the whole family as well.

The organist continued playing until the entire family had filed in and the congregation was seated. She could hear them behind her now, aunts, uncles, cousins, in-laws, friends, and colleagues all come to pay their last respects to her father. She couldn't remember seeing the parking lot of the church so full before. When the choir was finished singing *Blessed Assurance*, Shannon was startled to hear her name and the names of her family cementing her consciousness in the moment. Phillip had begun the funeral sermon.

"A man's worth is not measured in the size of his home. It is not measured by the dollars in his bank account nor the make of his car. No. It is not measured by any of these things.

"There is a far simpler way to measure a man's worth and Jimmy knew this fact all too well. For worth is measured by the state of a man's world when he leaves this earth. And Jimmy's world was left considerably better for him having been in it. His wife, Myrna, knows this well. His four children know this. His ten grandchildren know this.

"But he didn't limit this knowledge to his immediate family. His extended family, friends, coworkers, and anyone who came to know him were bettered by his actions. He made his entire world a much better place."

For the first time, Shannon began to hear the muffled sobs throughout the congregation. Her daddy, one of the most humble men she'd ever known had been great. Far greater than she'd ever realized. To her, he was just Daddy. To everyone else, he was a giant. Perhaps that's how it always is. You never truly know someone until you reflect back and realize how empty your life will be without them. Perhaps, she had taken for granted that her daddy would always be there, would live to see her child grow up and have a life of their own, would always be home working on some project or planting a garden, would always be there to give advice. She just never pictured her life without him in it. Even as a child, when she dreamed of adventure and moving away from this small town, she always thought he would be there when she came back home. But now she realized that was all a childish façade and her life would forever be changed.

Her attention turned as the choir struck up the first chords of one of his favorite hymns.

> Tempted and tried we're oft' made to wonder
> Why it should be thus all the day long

While there are others living about us
Never molested, though in the wrong.

Shannon stared ahead at the wreath of flowers to the right of the coffin. The colors blurred together. She could see her daddy in the same pew he always sat in singing along to the words.

Farther along we'll know all about it
Farther along we'll understand why
Cheer up my brothers, live in the sunshine
We'll understand it all by and by.

Daddy always loved the sunshine. A sunny day meant a good day of work. Robby picked the perfect spray for his coffin. It was filled with yellow roses, the color of sunshine, just like Daddy would have liked, just like he'd picked out for Mama's kitchen. The light shining on the roses seemed to highlight the wood inlay on his coffin. Daddy would have appreciated that detail as well. It was something he would have done in his woodworking.

And then she realized her daddy would never make anything again. Before she could regain her composure, a tear trickled down her cheek. She had promised herself she would be strong, she wouldn't weep openly. After all, she'd had months and months to prepare for this moment. She'd had plenty of time to cry. They all had. All through the chemo, all through the downward progression, they all knew the end was nigh. Yet now that the moment had arrived, it seemed too soon. It happened too quickly.

She couldn't think like that. He was in a better place now. She knew that. She believed that with all her heart. He wasn't in pain any longer and he had been at peace in the end. She wondered how long it would be until she found peace, until she no longer grieved for the gaping hole left in her heart. She suspected the answer would be an eternity.

Phillip gave the benediction prayer and motioned the ushers to come forward. The coffin was carried down the center aisle followed by Myrna and the children. Family members followed in precession. It took almost ten minutes to clear the entire church. Dylan rested his arm around Shannon's shoulder as they stared out of the limo to watch the crowd form and people make their way to their respective vehicles. Sirens of the police cars sounded briefly to stop the passing traffic and they were off. Shannon couldn't actually remember the ride to the cemetery. One minute, they were pulling out of the church parking lot, the next they were walking toward the open grave where the ushers and funeral staff were placing her father's coffin. She couldn't understand the words that Phillip was speaking. All she could do was to stare at the flowers. And then the crowd stood and started filing once more in front of the casket offering hugs to her, her Mom, and her siblings. She didn't remember who she hugged or what was said. Time and sound had ceased to exist.

Robby nudged her saying that it was time to go. She looked around and most of the crowd had left. Many were going back to the church to prepare a lunch for the entire family. Others had simply gone home. She looked at the casket one last time and reached out to trace the gold inlay around the edging.

"Goodbye, Daddy." She whispered and let Robby lead her to the car.

∽∾

The final days of October saw a bitter chill fall over the countryside. Autumn was in full swing and several of Myrna's neighbors had decorated their porches with pumpkins and gourds. Myrna had changed the wreath on her door with the season, the only outward decoration she felt energetic enough to make. After forty-three years of marriage, the house seemed eerily quiet. She'd spent so much time devoted to Jimmy's care in the last six months that she hadn't taken any time for herself. Now she had all the time in the world and no idea how to spend it; so she busied herself as best she could to try to fill the time.

She walked through her home, the home that Jimmy had insisted she have. It was still filled with so many of his things, his clothes, all his tools, his scent. It would take time to truly make it her home without him. She knew she needed to begin the process of going through his things, but that could wait a little while longer. She didn't have the energy for that today. She doubted she would have the energy for that for several more months. Those possessions, those things, were a part of him. A part of whom he had been and the thought of parting with anymore of Jimmy was more than she could bear on such a cold day.

Robby and Dylan had talked about coming over and helping her sort out some of his papers. While there was no immediate rush, she knew that project was more pressing because of the taxes she would have to settle in a few months time. She should really go through some of it before they came over. She didn't want to lose anything of any importance, anything that reminded her of him.

His desk was far more organized than any of the papers she normally kept and she began to sift through various expenses and receipts that her accountant would surely need. She found the receipts from the funeral home where he had made payments on his service. The first was dated almost five years prior. Jimmy had begun planning his funeral during the end of his first battle with cancer. Long before anyone else had thought of such details. Jimmy had known. He'd known all along. There were receipts for the house and maintenance records for the two vehicles. She set all that aside for Robby and Dylan to sort out.

Opening the side drawer, she was surprised to find an envelope with her name scribbled on the front in Jimmy's handwriting. She found his letter opener and carefully sliced open the top. Inside were a single sheet of paper and a picture of her standing under a tree.

Sept 29

Myrna,
I was sitting on the front porch this morning staring out at the mulberry tree in the front yard. It reminded me of long ago when you and I were first married. We walked through my dad's old farm until we

197

came to an old mulberry tree very much like the one we have now and you leaned against the bark without a care in the world. I took this picture of you standing beneath the mulberry tree and then picked one of the blossoms from a nearby flower and put it in your hair. You were the prettiest girl I'd ever seen. You still are.

I've kept that picture all these years and often think back on that day. All the plans we made and the hopes we had for the future. Some of those have come true. Some haven't. In many ways, my life has been far better than I could have ever imagined and you are the reason why.

I know we don't have much longer together, but I wanted you to know how much I love you. You have been the best partner any man can have and I hope you always remember that you've made me the happiest man on earth. I wouldn't change a thing or trade a minute that I've spent with you.

I love you and will be waiting for you until we meet again.

Love,
Jimmy

She stared at the picture she'd long ago forgotten and cried until she thought her heart would burst.

CRED

"Boy, something sure smells good."

Myrna looked up suddenly expecting to see Jimmy walking into the kitchen. But no, it was Dylan. He sounded so much like his father it could be startling sometimes. Right down to the very words Jimmy would have spoken. He was definitely his father's son.

"It's almost done. I'm just heating up the sweet potato soufflé now. Then we'll warm the rolls and be ready to eat." Myrna looked around the kitchen to make sure she hadn't missed anything.

"Sounds like we're going to eat good this year." Dylan smiled and wrapped his arm around his mom.

"I hope it's all good. If not, everybody will have to do without." Myrna was still working through her mental checklist.

"It's always good, Mama." He kissed her forehead. "You doing okay?"

"Yeah," she sighed. "I'm okay."

"Dylan, come over here and make yourself useful. Start slicing up the turkey so we can put it on the table." Emma directed.

"I think I can handle that." He released his mother and gave a quick hug to his sister who looked a tad frazzled at the moment.

Shannon came in bearing a broccoli casserole and homemade macaroni-and-cheese. "Hey, Mom. Where do you want these?"

"Anywhere you can find room on the table." Myrna answered through the growing crowd.

"I don't think there is any room left on the table." Shannon replied balancing a dish in each hand.

"Let me help you." Amy took one of the dishes from Shannon and they shifted several things around until they managed to squeeze everything onto the overstuffed table. The family had outdone themselves this year. There was enough food to feed a football team and still have leftovers.

Robby looked around the kitchen as the women hurriedly finalized the last of the Thanksgiving dinner, enlisting Dylan's help where needed. He reached into the freezer, pulled out the ice tray, and began filling plastic cups for the drinks. When the final tally was calculated, almost twenty cups were awaiting ownership. The entire family was gathered together. The only one missing was Daddy. The thought struck a bittersweet cord and Robby smiled despite himself knowing how much Dad would have loved to see everyone here today.

"You finished with those, Robby?" Shannon asked. The women had started gathering everyone to come and eat.

"Yep." He smiled over at his baby sister. "That's the last one."

"Okay, everybody come on. It's ready." Emma shepherded the crowd in.

"Who's going to say the blessing?" Myrna looked around. That too had always been Jimmy's job. Now, it fell to other shoulders.

"I'll say it." Dylan volunteered seeing his mother's face.

They bowed their heads as Dylan began. "Heavenly Father, we thank you today for the blessings you have given us and for the food we're about to receive. We thank you for allowing this family to visit with one another and for giving us all safe travels here. We pray that you'll keep all of us in your loving arms both today and through the rest of the year. Heal the hearts that are broken and comfort those today who are less fortunate. In your holy name we pray. Amen."

A collective Amen whispered through the family. The kids lined up first with plates ready for the feast. They would join their cousins at the kid's table in the sunroom. The adults would venture to the formal dining room and squeeze around the antique table.

Only a few would need to sit at the bar in the kitchen.

"If the family keeps growing, we'll need to rent out a convention hall." Dylan leaned over and whispered to Shannon.

She laughed. "I'll let you and Amy get to work on that one."

"On what?" Amy joined them.

"Dylan wants a bigger family." Shannon was laughing.

Some of the blood drained from Amy's face. "I didn't think you were going to say anything." She whispered to him.

Quick on the uptake, Shannon clued in on the silent exchange between them. "What?"

She peered at Amy. "You're not?"

"Kind of."

"Oh my gosh! That's great!" Shannon almost spilled her tea as she hugged her sister-in-law.

Everyone stopped in midair as excitement filled the room.

"What's going on?" Myrna didn't like being out in the dark on Thanksgiving.

"Amy's pregnant!" Shannon gushed releasing her and hugging Dylan with gusto.

"Pregnant?"

"Congratulations."

"When did you find out?"

"When is it due?"

202

The adults temporarily forgot the food upon hearing the news. They congratulated the happy couple and offered a fresh round of hugs, then proceeded to overfill their plates with food. The baby was due in late August, the hottest part of the year as the seasoned mothers pointed out. Right around Dylan's birthday. He was planning on adding a room onto their home for the nursery. Hopefully, he could get that started in the spring and have it well finished before Amy got too far along. Plans were discussed for clothes and furniture that would be needed. Shannon still had most of the furniture and all the old crib sheets that she used for Katie. They had hoped for a baby brother for Katie although he had yet to arrive. Actually, he wasn't even on the horizon. She would get all that together and bring it down. Emma had a rocker she never used and was planning on donating to Goodwill. It would go great in a nursery. Robby and Dylan discussed the technical aspects of the addition to the house. They could work together after the first of the year to draw up some blueprints and decide the best layout.

"Don't forget there's Chocolate Delight in the refrigerator for dessert." Myrna reminded them.

More than a few pairs of jeans fit snugly that afternoon as the dishes were cleared away and Styrofoam plates were prepared to take home. Around three o'clock, Shannon and Darren loaded up their car for the journey through Atlanta traffic. Hopefully, everyone else stayed out of town and the roads would be light but that was never a guarantee. Best to head out early just in case.

Amy began to look a little green around the gills. It was too much food and too much excitement for the first trimester. Dylan took her home to rest. Emma and Robby lingered late into the afternoon. Myrna enjoyed their company as they discussed Christmas and the upcoming New Year. A new year and a new addition to the family. It was a drastic change to the year they had all just endured. But then, life it seems has a way of evening out the chaos and confusion, the sorrow and sadness. Time may not erase the scars but it will knit the pieces back together again if only one stitch at a time.

Epilogue

A LOT HAS changed since that autumn. Only four short years after Daddy passed, the bottom fell out and we saw the worst economic crisis since the Great Depression. Property prices plummeted as millions of people lost their jobs and shortly thereafter their homes. Most of the pundits claimed it was a recession brought on by a market correction (whatever that means), but everyone I knew was thoroughly depressed, both economically and otherwise. I guess what you called it all depended on whether or not you kept your job and your home.

It was during this time that Mama found a lump in her breast. I don't mind saying that scared us all a pretty good bit, especially after watching what Daddy went through. She had a rough go of it for awhile but she's better now. Still not a hundred percent. Something to do with the long term preventative medicine she's on. It seems to rob her of a good bit of the stamina that she's enjoyed for so many years.

Thankfully, all she had to worry about was getting better and not taking care of a huge farm. Both my brothers were struggling to keep their businesses afloat and couldn't have helped out much during that time. It would have been a strain on everyone if she'd still had to take care of the old place. Daddy must have been a psychic. He knew before any of us seemed to that one day she would not be able to take care of all they had built together. And if she had tried to sell anything during that time, she would have been forced to take pennies on the dollar if she'd been able to sell at all. I guess the good Lord does look after us all if we have the sense to listen.

Our family managed to survive the financial woes although none of us came out completely unscathed. Robby downsized his construction business considerably and is only now showing any signs of recovery. He was extremely fortunate to endure since so many other commercial contractors in the state were forced to fold.

Dylan's business actually began to prosper during that time. No one could afford new cars so maintenance shops did very well. Unfortunately, he worked so hard during the first year of the recession that he tore his rotator cuff. Not having anyone to take over the business while he was out for surgery, he postponed the procedure and continued to work. By the time he had the problem corrected, the damage was significant and he was forced to quit auto work himself. He still runs the shop but only works in the office now. He's scaled back his workload but we all can tell how much he misses working with his hands. Emma and I are still gainfully employed at our same old jobs. Fortunately, we picked stable careers that are usually recession proof. We'll probably stay at our jobs until we retire or we win the lottery. I'm planning my retirement in about ten years.

Mom finally finished the last of her preventative treatments with a clean bill of health from the doctor. For that we are all truly grateful. It's hard to believe that next year marks ten years since we lost him. Even after all this time, I can still hear the stoic voice of the greatest man I shall ever know. And if I look closely at his old recliner, I can see the gentle flick of the evening paper as he peers around the side.

About the Book

Some stories are born through monumental sparks of inspiration, others through less exciting means. This work falls into the latter category. It all started thanks to a grand struggle to find the perfect Christmas present for my mom. She happens to own everything she wants and what she doesn't currently possess, she goes out and buys herself. There is simply nothing she wants or needs, which puts those of us shopping for her in a bit of a pickle.

The only thing I knew she didn't have was a novel based on the relationship she shared with my father. It is a project I'd thought about writing for many years but never felt truly ready to delve into the complexities and emotions that were required. This past Christmas, desperation finally overtook fear and I decided the time was right to explore this story.

For those of you who may be familiar with my family, you know the truth is far more interesting than the words that fill these pages. I hope you'll overlook the numerous creative liberties I've taken here.

For those who are experiencing this story for the first time, some of the events here were inspired by actual events. Other events were not. This is a work of fiction not of fact. As such, the names have been changed to protect the guilty. However, there are a few important facts that you should be aware of. Yes, I was lucky to have two wonderful parents. Although he had no degree, my dad was one of the smartest men I ever knew. And, emu steaks really are tough!

Thank you for reading. I hope you enjoy.

(P.S. Mom liked it!)

Thank you for reading!!

Dear Reader,

I hope you enjoyed **Beneath the Mulberry Tree**. I am truly honored that you chose to spend a few hours with the characters I love so much. I know how many wonderful stories there are and you choosing mine amid the thousands means more to me than words can say.

I'm currently working on my latest novel, 'Til the Stars Stop Shining, and would love to hear your feedback. Please feel free to contact me by email at AuthorJenniferBDuffey@gmail.com or on Facebook at www.facebook.com/authorJenniferBDuffey.

Lastly, I'd like to ask each and every one of you a huge favor. If you have a few extra minutes after reading this work, please leave a review on either Amazon.com and/or Goodreads.com. Whether you loved it, liked it, or hated it, your feedback is very important to me.

Again, thank you so much for spending a few hours with the people I call family and friends. I look forward to continuing our journey together for many years to come.

Kindest Regards,

Jennifer B Duffey

THE FACE
IN THE MIRROR

JENNIFER B. DUFFEY

Chapter One

A SLIVER OF light peeked through the breach in the curtains, landing squarely in Carmen's eye and awakening the demon drumming in her head. It had been a great night, the perfect end to the last week of freedom before the semester began. Unfortunately, it was a night that involved far too little sleep. Her final year of college was a time of great celebration.

It was also a week she was desperately trying to forget.

She turned her head to avoid any further onslaught of morning illumination and glanced at the digital clock on her nightstand. Just after nine. She'd actually slept for almost five hours. Longer than she slept after many a wild night although she had hoped to get to bed much earlier. Five hours would do today. Her schedule was clear except for making sure her new roommate got settled in. Nothing major there. Carmen had already shown her where everything was and where she could store her stuff. It was simply a matter of answering any questions the girl might have and then the day would be free and clear for laundry, rest, and recovery.

What was her name again? Mindy? Maddy? Oh God, Carmen's head pounded louder the harder she thought.

"Maggie. That was it," she mumbled to the empty room. She massaged her scalp to try and relieve some of the pressure from her exertion.

Slowly her new roommate's face came clearer into focus. A curtain of dark hair hung limply down past Maggie's shoulders hiding much of her face and any distinguishable features. The girl wore thick framed glasses, the kind that hipsters were bringing back in vogue. On Maggie they completed a wall between a frightened child and the rough and tumble world outside. Carmen had been stunned when she happened to glance into a pair of dazzling emerald eyes hidden beneath the veil of eyewear and hair. It was a momentary pass into a world otherwise hidden from view.

Carmen slapped the alarm to silence the annoying buzz, knocking it to the floor in the process. Nine thirty. Her designated time to be out of bed. Well, maybe five more minutes wouldn't hurt.

Of course, if everything had gone according to plan, she wouldn't have needed to find a new roommate under such urgent circumstances. What should have been a phenomenal beginning to her senior year of college almost ended with crisis and panic. Sandra, her best friend since grade school, was supposed to move in and split the cost of the off campus apartment. The two planned everything down to the last detail over the summer. Things were set in stone until Thursday when Sandra called in a state of hysteria. Her parents were separating after twenty-two years of marriage. Her father had moved out to live with his mistress. Her mother was beside herself with despair. On top of everything, there was great concern about the financial stability of her father's company. His partners believed the books were considerably shorter than they should be. The word embezzlement hadn't actually been used but it had been hinted at. Heavily. There was simply no money for her to continue her education so far away from home even if it was an excellent school like Hamilton University. She was transferring to a local college to help her mom sort through the chaos.

They had dreamed of going to Hamilton since their junior year of high school when a rather handsome coed stood outside the cafeteria handing out fliers to the little out of the way school. The pictures were stunning. Nestled in the mountains just north of Hiawassee, Georgia, it was a world away from the cotton fields of Perry. They could picture themselves sitting along the banks of Chatuge Lake like the girls smiling from the brochures. When they realized that Hamilton had both an outstanding journalism program for Sandra and top notch prelaw curriculum for Carmen, the pair was hooked on the idea of heading north to further their education. Now those plans were torn asunder. Their final year of collegiate study would be spent apart.

Carmen was at a complete loss. Sandra's parents had always seemed so loving and perfect for one another. She desperately wanted to be there for her friend and second mom. She couldn't begin to imagine what they must be going through. Then, as she hung up the phone, she realized their crisis led directly to a crisis for her. She'd only budgeted half of the room and board for this apartment. That, in itself, had been a struggle. She had nothing extra to pay the other half. Her financial resources were already strained beyond the limit.

The following morning, she hung hastily made flyers on every campus bulletin board she could find. Calls started coming in by noon. The first three calls she rejected outright. She simply wasn't interested in underclassmen looking for a place to party every night or shack up with their beaus. Those callers reeked of drama.

The fourth caller introduced herself as Maggie Arnet, a junior studying information technology. Maggie was a sharp contrast to the previous applicants. When asked about boyfriends, she stammered, "No. I'm not seeing anyone. I'm single."

"Where are you living now?"

"I'm in the dorms." Maggie replied.

Carmen had experienced those less than satisfactory living conditions. "Yeah, the dorms suck, don't they?"

"Well, I've only been here for a week. I just transferred from Armstrong. I was living at home there."

"Didn't take you long to decide." Carmen chuckled.

Maggie was hesitant. "It's just that everybody is so loud here. Maybe it'll be better once the term begins but I'm really used to a calmer environment."

That was a good sign in a potential roomy. Once the term began, Carmen had to focus strictly on her studies. It was the only way to ensure her acceptance into law school. They met later that evening to discuss rent and utilities. Papers were signed. The deposit was given. Maggie would move in the next day.

"What about all those housing fees for the dorms?" Carmen wanted to make sure this new girl could hold up the financial obligation she was signing on for.

"The housing office told me that as long as I move out of the dorm before the start of term, I could get a refund. All I've got to do is turn the form back in tomorrow and I'll get the refund in a couple of weeks." Maggie explained.

It was almost too good to be true yet Carmen wasn't going to question her luck. Snatching prosperity from the jaws of certain defeat provided the perfect reason to join her fellow seniors for one last pre-term celebration. Now her body rebelled against the simple task of moving from the bed to the bathroom. She glanced at the clock once again. 9:52. She shouldn't delay any longer. She rubbed her head and grunted loudly as she sat up on the edge of her bed. It was a tricky maneuver. For a brief moment, she feared she might lose the meal she'd eaten the night before. A meal she couldn't completely remember but one she was in no hurry to revisit.

She showered until the water turned from scalding to tepid, allowing the steam and spray to relax her aching muscles. By the time she toweled off, she felt almost human albeit far from one hundred percent. She sipped a glass of water while the coffee brewed and lightly toasted some bread. Somehow she didn't think she could tolerate the overly sugared cereal she commonly kept atop the refrigerator.

By the time Maggie arrived an hour later, Carmen had already started a load of laundry and was nursing her third cup of coffee.

"Good morning," Maggie greeted.

"Morning," Carmen returned, grimacing as the late morning sun burst through the open doorway.

"Are you okay?"

"Just have a headache." She moved out of the direct line of sunlight to a darker corner of the room.

Maggie nodded but said nothing else as she began to unpack her car, heaving the first of several large boxes through the living room. Carmen had hoped their next door neighbor, Tom, would see Maggie and come to the rescue, thereby relieving her of any guilt for not assisting. That way she wouldn't be forced to brave the sunlight. Apparently, this wasn't going to happen.

"How many more trips do you have to make?" Carmen asked, against the advice of her still aching body.

"Five or six maybe."

She couldn't let the poor girl struggle alone. "Let me get my shoes on and I'll help you."

Maggie almost dropped the box she was carrying.

"You okay?" Carmen grabbed her arm to steady her from the fall.

"Yeah. Just lost my footing. Thanks."

"Well, whatever you do, don't fall and break your leg. I don't want to carry all your stuff up those stairs." Carmen laughed at her own joke as she slipped on her sneakers.

"Yeah, that wouldn't be good, would it?" Maggie mumbled scurrying to her new bedroom to deposit her things. When she returned, Carmen had donned a ball cap to hide her less than fashionable hairstyle. Her hair pulled through the back in a loose ponytail.

"Come on. Let's go get your stuff." She said motioning Maggie forward.

"Okay."

They were debating the best way to carry a rather awkward and bulky box when Tom arrived with a friend. Carmen's face split into a wide smile as they exited his Honda Civic.

"Perfect timing as ever!" She greeted.

"Not sure I like the sound of that." He smiled.

Maggie felt her end of the box being lifted easily out of her hands and looked up to see the friend smiling down at her.

"Hi," he said.

"Hi," she stammered back.

"Okay, sweetness. Where does this thing go?" Tom asked now holding Carmen's end of the box as the guys began to trek up the stairs.

"The bedroom beside mine." She replied and dove into the car for more boxes. She emerged balancing several items on a mini ironing board.

"Looks like we just cut those six trips down considerably." Her smile was infectious.

"Yeah." Maggie watched her roommate climb the stairs before grabbing her most prized possession and following suit.

"You play the violin?" Tom asked, surveying the case and the sheets of music that protruded from the top of the box she carried.

"It's a viola actually." She clambered to her room to put the box down.

Carmen was stacking the boxes on top of each other by size so Maggie had room to maneuver in the confined area.

"You can go ahead and start unpacking if you want. The guys said they'd get the last couple of things."

"Really?" The question slipped out before Maggie realized it.

"Yep. Do you need any help?"

"Um . . . no. I've got it, thanks." Maggie spluttered.

"No problem. How long have you played?" Carmen asked pointing to the viola case.

"Oh, since I was a kid." She looked down at her hands instinctively.

"Wow. You must be pretty good. Are you in the orchestra on campus?"

Maggie gave a nervous laugh and shook her head. "Oh no. I'm nowhere near that good."

"I bet you're great, but if you decide to play in the apartment just remember we have to keep things down after eleven p.m."

"Okay."

"Here's the rest of the stuff." Tom announced, walking through the door and plopping a handful of miscellaneous items on the bed. His friend was right behind him carrying his own load of treasures.

"We didn't see anything else."

"Is that everything?" Carmen turned to Maggie to inquire.

"That's it. Thanks." Maggie managed to string the words together in an almost coherent sentence.

Carmen finally took the opportunity to introduce Tom to her new roommate.

"This is my best friend, Jeff." Tom introduced the fourth member of the party.

"Are you in the pre-law program? I think we had a class together last semester." Jeff asked Carmen.

"McMurray's Poli-Sci class?"

"Yeah." Jeff nodded.

"I thought you looked familiar." Carmen smiled.

Maggie noticed his eyes lingered on Carmen's sun kissed smile. She had seen that look all too often and suddenly felt like the self-conscious third wheel. She desperately searched for a way to exit the situation but as this was her room, she was unsure which way to go.

Carmen came to the rescue. "Come on, guys. We better let Maggie get settled in. Let me know if you need any help."

Maggie stood there alone in her bedroom looking around. It had certainly been a huge help to have Carmen and her friends carry most of the things up. She hadn't expected that. When she unpacked at the dorms, the other girls barely looked up from their movie to acknowledge her existence. They didn't even notice she'd walked into the room. It was the same when she left. She honestly doubted if they knew her name.

Since moving in here this morning, she'd already said more than she had during her entire stay at the dorms. That wasn't overly surprising. She wasn't known as a talker. Still, this newfound camaraderie was unsettling. She wanted to cradle her viola and calm her nerves with a beloved sonata. Yet she couldn't. Carmen and the guys were loudly joking in the living room. She couldn't bring herself to play while they were so close by. She didn't want to hear their jeers. She would have to wait until they left.

There was little doubt that both of those guys would want to take Carmen out for lunch. She was, after all, a classic beauty. Brown locks that cascaded past her shoulders. Bright brown eyes highlighted with tiny golden flecks. A body that could grace the cover of any magazine. By any conservative definition, Carmen was stunning.

Maggie decided she would find her calm when they left to find lunch and whatever the afternoon held. In the meantime, she set about unpacking her belongings into the room that would be her home for the next year. Her wardrobe, limited as it was, quickly found a place in the closet and chest-of-drawers. Carmen had explained that this was one of the last furnished apartments in town and the furnishings had been sparse indeed.

"I can't believe they don't even have a full length mirror in the bedrooms." Carmen had vented when Maggie signed the lease.

"It shouldn't be a problem." Maggie couldn't explain how relieved that piece of information made her. Not to someone like Carmen who was obviously used to preening in front of a mirror.

Maggie pushed the thought from her mind and continued unpacking. After making her bed and putting the remaining linens on the shelf in her closet, she unfolded her laptop and placed it on the desk opposite her bed. It really needed to charge. She crawled around on the floor before realizing the plug was on the base of the lamp for easier access. A few moments later, the legal pads and pens she used to jot notes were neatly arranged beside her Hewlett Packard. Most of the other miscellaneous items fit neatly in the closet. The oversized stuffed rabbit sat in a place of honor beside her pillow. That left the viola, music stand, and sheet music. She thought once again about playing; but, she could still hear their laughter echoing through the apartment. Best to wait until they left. It shouldn't be long now.

She decided instead to fire up her computer and surf the web. Finally after more than an hour of mindless browsing, she heard a knock at the door. That was strange. She expected them to just leave.

"Come in." She didn't realize that Carmen had already swung the door open and was halfway through the entrance.

"Hey, what do you like on your pizza?"

"What?" Maggie was confused.

"We're ordering pizza. What do you like?" Carmen clarified.

"Um. . . pepperoni is fine. I guess." She couldn't believe they were staying in.

"You guess? Do you like pepperoni or not?" Carmen pressed.

"It's okay. It's fine."

Carmen was unconvinced. "What kind of pizza do you like?"

"Cheese." Maggie cowered slightly under the weight of Carmen's stare.

"Then why did you say pepperoni?"

Maggie didn't know how to respond. She couldn't remember the last time anyone had asked her what type of pizza she wanted. Sure, she'd ordered things for herself, but when groups of people were involved, she usually fell in line with the majority opinion. There was no use in ordering something special just for her.

"I …um…just didn't want you to go to any trouble."

"What trouble? We're ordering pizza not making a five course meal."

"I guess I thought you had already ordered." Maggie tried to smooth the air.

"Why in the world would we do that without asking you first, silly?" Carmen countered.

Maggie could feel the air escaping the room at a rapid rate. The temperature rose palpably. She wanted nothing more than to shut the world away and hear the haunting notes of a concerto. She hastily struggled for words to answer Carmen's accusations.

"Um…"

Carmen watched her for a moment more.

"Whatever." She shrugged her shoulder still baffled at Maggie's response.

"Anyway, I'm glad you're finished unpacking. We need a fourth for our trivial pursuit game. The guys are talking smack about how much smarter they are, so we need to kick their butts good."

Maggie sat opened mouthed.

"Come on." Carmen reached for her hand and pulled her to her feet. "I know you're shy and all, but I'm not taking no for an answer. I'm not letting them get the best of me."

Maggie stumbled slightly as she followed, or was rather dragged, into the living room where the guys were setting up the board game.

"Okay, Maggie wants a cheese pizza." Carmen draped her arm loosely over the girl's shoulder.

"And she said we're going to destroy you guys!" She added for good measure.

Maggie turned paler than a snowman in winter. She looked around the room until her knees began to give way and she quickly sat down hoping to vanish from view.

Tom laughed. "The key to intimidation, Maggie, is not to pass out before the game begins."

"It's okay, Maggie. We'll take it easy on you gals." Jeff added.

That fired Carmen up again. "You will not!"

"It's obvious you two are outmatched." Tom plucked at the exposed nerve.

"Shut up and order the pizza. Then prepare to get spanked."

"Well, if you insist." Jeff grinned broadly.

Carmen glared at him furiously but she had to admit she was at a distinct disadvantage. Maggie appeared to be near hyperventilation. God help them if she actually had to answer a question. The poor thing might melt into a puddle of mush right in the middle of the floor.

Soon the game was afoot. Carmen easily answered her sports question. How many events are there in a decathlon? Ten, of course. Tom was less fortunate with his sports question. How many squares are on a chess board?

"Fifty? I don't know." He shrugged.

Carmen laughed.

"Sixty-four." Maggie whispered.

The others fell silent in shock that the mouse had spoken.

"That's right. How'd you know that?" Carmen was genuinely interested.

"I play on the computer." Maggie fidgeted with her hands.

"Hah!" Carmen waved her arms at the two gents. "BAM! We're gonna win!"

The game quickly evened up with a series of easy questions. Who was the housekeeper for the Brady household? Who lost the 1980 Presidential election? Name the March sisters. Both teams were only one piece away when the girls were asked what Joseph Priestley discovered in 1774?

"1774? Who the heck is Joseph Priestley? I thought that was the guy from 90210." Carmen huffed.

"Hah! One piece left. Can you answer if or not?" Tom could smell the victory in the air.

Carmen looked around frantically.

"Oxygen." Maggie stammered.

Jeff flipped the card over quickly. "That's right."

"HAH!" Carmen jumped up and began an impromptu victory dance of no real form. Then she hugged Maggie roughly around the shoulders. Maggie couldn't help but laugh as Carmen began dancing again to the chant of "We won! We won! Ha ha! We won!"

The fellows were less excited.

"That was a lucky guess." Jeff insisted.

"I think you two cheated somehow." Tom avowed.

"Face it, boys! We kicked your butts. BAM!" Carmen wouldn't let it go.

"I demand a rematch!" Tom was equal to the challenge.

"Set up the board." Carmen countered.

Jeff came to the rescue. "Aren't you supposed to be meeting Lisa in a little while?"

"What?" Tom looked at the clock on his phone. "Oh, yeah."

He turned his attention back to Carmen. "This isn't over."

"Anytime, baby." She retorted. "Anytime."

They glared at each other in competitive fury. Tom blinked first, knowing he was on the verge of tardiness for his date with his fiancée. It brought a fresh smile from Carmen.

Jeff grabbed him by the elbow. "Let's go before you two start arm wrestling."

Tom picked up his keys from the entertainment center. "No mercy for the rematch."

"You're still going to lose."

"Come on, tough guy." Jeff pulled his friend along. "Carmen, see you in class Monday."

"Bright and early."

"Maggie, nice to meet you." Jeff remarked. "By the way, you have a beautiful smile. You should wear it more often."

They were gone.

Maggie felt her face ignite. She hadn't even realized she'd been smiling.

Get your copy of

THE FACE IN THE MIRROR

Available on Amazon today!!

Made in the USA
San Bernardino, CA
01 September 2019